Frankie & Lexi 2

Luvin' A Young Beast

Tina J

Copyright 2018

More Books by Tina J

A Thin Line Between Me & My Thug 1-2
I Got Luv for My Shawty 1-2
Kharis and Caleb: A Different kind of Love 1-2
Loving You is a Battle 1-3
Violet and the Connect 1-3
You Complete Me
Love Will Lead You Back
This Thing Called Love
Are We in This Together 1-3
Shawty Down to Ride For a Boss 1-3
When a Boss Falls in Love 1-3
Let Me Be The One 1-2
We Got That Forever Love
Ain't No Savage Like The One I got 1-2
A Queen & Hustla 1-2 (collab)
Thirsty for a Bad Boy 1-2
Hasaan and Serena: An Unforgettable Love 1-2
We Both End Up With Scars
Caught up Luvin a beast 1-3
A Street King & his Shawty 1-2
I Fell for the Wrong Bad Boy 1-2 (collab)
Addicted to Loving a Boss 1-3
All Eyes on the Crown 1-3
I Need that Gangsta Love 1-2 (collab)
Still Luvin' a Beast 1-2
Creepin' With The Plug 1-2
I Wanna Love You 1-2
Her Man, His Savage 1-2
When She's Bad, I'm Badder 1-3
Marco & Rakia 1-3
Feenin' for a Real One 1-3
A Kingpin's Dynasty 1-3
What Kind Of Love Is This?
Frankie & Lexi

Warning:

This book is strictly Urban Fiction and the story is **NOT**

REAL!

Characters will not behave the way you want them to; nor will

they react to situations the way you think they should. Some of

them may be drug addicts, kingpins, savages, thugs, rich, poor,

ho's, sluts, haters, bitter ex-girlfriends or boyfriends, people

from the past and the list can go on and on. That is what Urban

Fiction mostly consists of. If this isn't anything you foresee

yourself interested in, then do yourself a favor and don't read it

because it's only going to piss you off. □□

Also, the book will not end the way you want so please be

advised that the outcome will be based solely on my own

thoughts and ideas. I hope you enjoy this book that y'all made

me write. Thanks so much to my readers, supporters, publisher

and fellow authors and authoress for the support. □□

Author Tina J

Previously...

Lexi

"What's wrong?" Frankie asked when I woke up in a sweat. I had fallen asleep after Dree and SJ left. I didn't even wait up for the pizza because the medication kicked right in. I looked at my phone and it was after ten.

"Something's wrong." I stood up too fast and got dizzy.

"What you mean." He came over and had me sit back down.

"Where's SJ?" I started panicking.

"SJ is at the house with Dree."

"You sure?" He looked at me.

"Yes. Don't you remember they left here together? Its why we have lil man for the night."

"Oh yea. Can you call and make sure he's ok?"

"Lexi, what's going on?"

"I don't know Frankie. I was asleep and my body jumped and woke me up. Its like it told me to wake up because something terrible happened. The only time I had this before is when SJ got hit by a car." I remembered that shit like yesterday.

I was home sick as hell and him and Frankie were out riding their bikes like always. My mom gave me some medicine that put me to sleep. Outta nowhere, I woke up from my sleep like I just did and knew shit wasn't right. I kept asking if everyone was ok and my parent told me yes. A half hour later my aunt Essence called and said SJ was hit by a car and in the hospital.

Its like because we were so close, when something happened to the other we could feel it. The same thing happened when I broke my arm. SJ was home and felt something was wrong and when he found out, we both thought it was weird since we weren't twins. But when you're that close with someone I guess it happens.

"He's not answering but when I called Dree, she said he's outside talking to your uncle."

"That's weird."

"Lexi, I know all about your gut so let's hope its wrong." I nodded and he kissed my forehead.

"I hope its wrong too but the feeling is too strong." The doorbell rang and I both went to answer it. Frankie said he was going downstairs in the basement. We both knew only someone from the family was at the door.

"How you feeling sis?" My brother asked when he stopped by with Raya. After she told her father what happened he contacted the school and told them his daughter was transferring closer to home ASAP. Of course, they claimed he couldn't get his money back or some shit but I don't think he really cared about that.

"I'm ok. Waiting to get this stupid cast off."

"How long do you have to wear it?" Raya asked and sat next to me.

"Four to six weeks and I'm dying with it on. I can't do anything."

"Do you need help around the house?" I looked at her and saw pure innocence in her eyes. Lord, I hope my brother doesn't hurt her.

"No thanks. My mom stops by and Frankie helps. What's up with you two? What made y'all stop by?"

"Your brother wanted to see Frankie."

"This late?" I questioned.

"It ain't that late and who cares?" He always had something smart to say.

"He's downstairs." Kane pecked her lips and strolled down the steps.

"Sooooo. Did he meet your father?" She put her head down.

"Ummm ok. Does he know about Kane?" She shook her head no.

"Raya you can't be in a relationship with him and hide at the same time. My brother isn't gonna stand for that much longer."

"What do you mean?"

"He obviously likes you a lot because he introduced you to me and wants to do the same with my parents. How do you think he's gonna feel that he can't do the same with you?"

"It's different with my dad." She started tearing up.

"I'm in love with Kane and as young as I am, I would love to spend the rest of my life with him. I also know he's a man and may not be able to stay faithful, which is why I don't wanna introduce him to my parents yet. What if he cheats? Then I'm stuck explaining why we broke up and then my dad can say, *I told you so*." She wiped her eyes.

"Honey you can't live your life under the what if's. Trust me. I've been there and done that. All it did was give me heartache after heartache. You have to live in the now and whatever is meant to be, will be. If you love my brother the way you say then show him off to everyone. Don't hide him because there's a woman or should I say women, who wouldn't hesitate to do what you're not."

"Do you think he's gonna cheat on me?"

"I don't think so but let me tell you this." I put my hand on hers.

"My father is very big on loyalty whether it comes to the streets, his family or his woman. He told all of us that when you fall in love make sure you give them everything you have to offer. Make them see no one else in the world can make him or her feel the way you can. And treat that person, the way you would treat your husband or wife. Because when everyone is gone, your spouse will still be by your side. And believe it or not, my brother has never called anyone his woman so if he's saying it about you, it says a lot."

"You think so?"

"I know so." She gave me a hug and asked where the bathroom is to clean her face. My brother came walking in with Frankie.

"Where's Raya?"

"In the bathroom."

"She good?" He gave me the side eye.

"Yea fool. Make sure you treat her right."

"I am. She's gonna be my wife." He looked in her direction and smiled.

"Really?" I was excited for my brother.

"Yup. Plus, ain't no other nigga touching that good ass pussy she got in between her legs." Frankie mushed him in the head.

"She's still my cousin."

"Do I say that when you mentioning how my sister has you moaning with some of the things she does?"

"FRANKIE!"

"What? You do and I can't wait until you're better and I can..."

"Bye y'all." Kane grabbed Raya and walked out. I hope she listened to me and tells her father about my brother because I can see a whole lot going wrong if she doesn't.

"Did the feeling go away?"

"No. I'm gonna drive to my aunt's house and see for myself."

"The hell you are."

"Frankie, I have to see if SJ is ok. I won't believe it until I see him with my own eyes."

"Aight. Let me get lil man. Go wait in the truck." I kissed his lips, opened the front door and came face to face with my worst nightmare. How the fuck did he know where I lived?

"If you scream, I'll kill you on this doorstep." I let the tears fall down my eyes. He snatched me up by my other arm and led me to a truck. When I got in, he pushed me inside and boy was I surprised.

"Crystal?" He closed the door and pulled off. *What in the hell is going on?*

Kane Jr.

Hearing that nigga had my sister only made shit worse. My cousin and uncle were possibly lying in the morgue, my sister was missing and in the care of a nigga whose pops molested her. What else could go wrong?

I hopped in my truck and drove to the hospital with my parents to drop my mom off. My dad refused to allow her to ride along to get Lexi and I didn't blame him. There's no way any of us would allow her to be placed in harm's way.

Frankie kept blaming himself and my father told him to stop. Someone had to tell him where they lived because the house was literally in the boondocks. The two of them wanted to be away from everyone and it's the reason they got it so far.

"Are you here to identify the Anderson men?" Some doctor asked and you saw my pops eyes getting watery. He may not fuck with my uncle but that's still his brother and nephew.

"Yes. I mean no. Kane, I can't go back there." My aunt was a mess.

"Essence, I have to meet this nigga to get Lexi."

"But I can't go back there. I don't wanna see him like that." She cried in my dad's arms and my mom rubbed her back.

"Frankie did he send the address yet?"

"Not yet and the number was blocked so I can't call him." All of a sudden you saw Dree's parents and Frankie's parents coming through the door. Another couple walked in and the guy was huge and he appeared to be worried. His wife or girlfriend had tears running down her face and was a nervous wreck.

"FUCK!" My pops shouted and I heard Frankie's mom call him over.

"Son are you ok? What happened?" He told them and his father and my pops went to speak in the corner.

"Uncle Hurricane why you here?" I turned when Frankie asked. I never met Raya's parents and here we are in a fucked-up situation and I'm face to face with them. I wonder where she is.

"Raya was in a car accident and they don't know if she's gonna make it." It was like someone knocked the wind outta me.

"What you mean if she makes it?" Frankie asked and looked at me.

"The cops said a truck ran a red light and hit her car. It flipped a few times. If she dies…" He stopped talking to get himself together. Her mom was on the chair hysterical crying.

"What do you mean a truck hit her?" I asked and his uncle looked at me.

"Who the fuck are you?" I was about to answer but my mom pulled me back. He squinted his eyes at me.

"Wait a minute. You're the nigga in the video. Did you send me that shit?" He moved closer to me.

"What video?"

"The video of you fucking her." My mom covered her mouth and it was like everything went from bad to worse.

I saw this nigga coming in with Lexi in front of him and pointing a gun in our direction.

"Lexi?" Everyone turned to look. He had her in front of him as he started talking shit. Just like that, things gotta outta hand real quick.

"APRIL NOOOOOOOOO." My father shouted. I guess when I asked what else could go wrong, this is it.

Lexi

I sat in the truck behind this dumb bitch who couldn't stop staring at me. She appeared to be in tip top shape besides the shiner clearing up under her eye. That shit happened over two weeks ago and it was still showing. I guess being light skinned doesn't pay off when it comes to bruises.

I rolled my eyes and this bitch reached in the back and smack the fuck outta me. Rome grabbed her shoulder and forced her to face front. My face was stinging but I had a trick for her ass.

I sat there quietly trying to figure out, how the hell are they even associated with one another? I felt my phone vibrating in my pocket but couldn't reach it because of this damn cast. I'm sure it was Frankie tryna figure out where I was, especially; when he told me to wait in the truck.

For most of the ride, neither of them said two words to each other or me. I paid it no mind because I was thinking of ways to get outta here. At this point, I didn't even care if he pushed me out while its moving. I just wanted to be away from this maniac. I tried the door knowing the safety locks were on it, but you can never be too sure. I even made an attempt to slide in the trunk and try to open it from the inside but nope. The second my body slid a little over the seat, Rome snatched my ass back down.

"Try that shit again and I'll blow your head off." He said with venom and a gun in my face. Crystal thought the shit was hilarious so of course, I smacked the shit outta her from the back and kept doing it until he stopped the truck and I jerk forward. I was even more mad this cast stopped me from choking her stupid ass.

"Yo, calm the fuck down." Crystal was in the front screaming like I was killing her.

"Fuck that bitch. She smacked me first and you didn't say shit to her." I complained like a child who didn't get their way.

"Really Lexi?" He questioned and sucked his teeth.

"Damn right. You know I'm half capacitated, thanks to you and she hit me." The bitch turned around and stuck her finger up.

"Very mature." I rolled my eyes.

"That may not be but this is." She unzipped Rome's pants and literally started to give him head. *Who the fuck does that?* And his dumb ass sat right there and let her.

"Is it good Rome? I mean is she doing it the way you like?" He glanced in the rearview mirror and smirked. He pushed her down further and pulled over. You could hear her gagging and I swore she was gonna vomit. Yet; the whole time he was staring at me.

"Oh Fuckkkkk!" He moaned and you could see Crystal tryna get up but he made her swallow every drop. She sat up and wiped her mouth.

"Feel better Crystal?"

"Very."

"Lexi. Come to the front and get me right."

"Nigga, is you crazy?" I shouted and Crystal looked at him.

"Rome, you are not about to disrespect me and ask that bitch to fuck you after I sucked you off."

"Why not. Her shit good as hell. Maybe that's why the nigga ain't with you now." She folded her arms and slammed her body against the seat.

"Rome take me home please." He zipped his jeans up and pulled back onto the highway.

"Nah, I got plans for you."

"Why though? I've never done anything to you."

"You really have no idea who I am, do you?"

"I know you're Rome Lyons who pretended to attend the same college as me. We were a couple for a few years, had a lotta fun together and once I came home for spring break, all your secrets came out. Like having kids and another woman." He sucked his teeth at the mention of his kids. I wonder if he's a deadbeat.

"Rome, why didn't you at least tell me you had kids? I still would've been with you but all this that you're doing is crazy." He stared at me in the rearview mirror.

"Nope. You have no idea who I am." He ignored everything I said.

My phone started vibrating again and his rang out loud. He picked it up and at first, I couldn't hear what the person said because Crystal was bitching about him wanting to fuck me. After she shut the fuck up, I heard another male voice on the other end discussing something concerning my cousin and uncle. I wasn't clear on the exact thing that happened but whoever it was, did some fucked up shit to them. I just broke down crying because even though I don't know what went down, my instinct was correct.

"What you crying for?" Crystal asked when the truck stopped. I wiped my eyes and looked out the window to see where we were, which was at a damn stop light.

"Is there a reason you're talking to me? I don't like you and you don't like me, soooooo." I asked and waited for her to answer.

"I could care less what you do or don't like. I'm only here because my man wanted me to show him where Frankie lived." She smiled.

"Hold on. You told him where he lived? How the hell did you even know about our spot?"

"Welllllll, the day you and your ghetto ass friend jumped me at the club." She tried to say and I corrected her quick.

"Jumped?" I busted out laughing.

"Bitch, you got your ass beat. We didn't need to jump your punk ass." Rome was shaking his head. He had hung the phone up after telling the person to meet him at the hospital because who he was looking for would be there.

"Whatever." She waved her hand and finished spitting some bullshit.

"Like I was saying before I was rudely interrupted." She was getting on my fucking nerves.

"I went home to put ice on my eye and come up with a plan to kill you." I shook my head at her ignorance. She is a big ass punk and talking about killing someone.

"I figured after you were shot, Frankie would be at the hospital and take you home when you were discharged, therefore; I waited."

"You stayed at the hospital for all those days?"

"Yup. I didn't have anything else to do." She shrugged her shoulders like being a stalker is ok.

"Now will you keep quiet so I can finish my story? I hate when people ask you something and keep interrupting." This bitch is fucking looney.

"The day I saw Frankie coming out with you, I followed at a safe distance and for a minute thought about saying forget it. But then I remembered how much I hated you. I admit the ride was pretty long and if you're not looking for the house, you will definitely miss it." She gave me a fake smile. I wanted to say, to keep your crazy ass away but her stupidity was entertaining.

"Low and behold, he pulled in and helped you out. I wanted to throw up in my mouth watching the amount of affection he showed you. I mean you left him, he moved on with other women and settled down with me. Why did you have to come back?"

"Crystal, if you knew how he felt about me, why get caught up in your feelings? Its never been a time when I called Frankie that he hadn't answered. You and all the other women hated me for no reason. I couldn't control what he did, how he treated y'all or if he chose you. And how did you end up with Rome anyway?"

"Oh that's easy." She said excitedly.

"I spotted him a few days later in a store and asked if he remembered me. Of course, he didn't but I did remind and give him a little something to make sure he never forgets me."

"Oh like a blow job in the truck?"

"You have to keep the relationship spicy." She smiled and ran her hand down his face. He moved out the way and she gave him a look.

"Y'all in a relationship Rome?"

"Hell no." I couldn't help but laugh. This bitch is delusional as fuck and was making up relationships in her head.

"ROME!" She shouted and the truck stopped.

"Get yo petty ass out my truck." She sucked her teeth.

"Call me later baby." I heard through the window that was rolled down. He pulled off without saying a word. *She has to be the dumbest bitch I know.*

"Why are you doing this Rome?" He made eye contact with me through the rearview mirror and remained quiet. Before I realized it, we were pulling up to the hospital. He hopped out the truck and came over to my side.

"Why are we here?" He snatched me out with the good arm and gripped it so tight, he had to be cutting off circulation.

"Shut the fuck up."

"Who you talking to?"

"You bitch. Now let's get this party started." Two black trucks pulled up and a bunch of guys jumped out, dressed in black and with weapons in their hands. It looked like they were dressed for war and once we stepped inside, I knew exactly what was about to happen.

This punk pulled me in front of him after speaking to the dudes and pushed me through the door. No one noticed us at first because it seemed like everyone was in their own conversation. My mom and brother were speaking to some man. My father was in the corner with Frankie's and Dree was sitting with her parents on the other side of the waiting room.

25

Why are they all here and how did he even know where to find them?

"Lexi?" Kane Jr. said and all hell broke loose.

Rome

I yanked this bitch out the truck and placed her in front of me just in case someone came out shooting. Hell yea, I'm using her as my shield. Won't none of those motherfuckers shoot if she's in the way. If you're wondering how I found out the person I want is at the hospital, I can thank my baby mom for it. She was leaving there, because her wound was infected and had to be checked. She said two of the guys who came in her house were in the emergency room but she didn't know why.

When she told me that nigga barged in her house, killed everyone and kept her alive, I knew he was aware of me being the one who shot Lexi. I don't really care if he killed the bitch because I was leaving her anyway. She loved pussy more than dick and, in the beginning, I was all for it but when she started calling me the chick name while fucking, I was over it. I am pissed he did the shit while my kids were in the house though.

"Y'all ready?" I asked my crew and the new dude who had to be in on shit.

"Hell yea. Let's get these motherfuckers." He was corny as hell but I'm impressed that he was able to get SJ. Unfortunately, Frankie wasn't with him but it's all good because they're here now.

"Let's go." I moved my hand from Lexi's arm and wrapped it around her waist.

"Look at this. Your entire family is here." I whispered in her ear and kissed her cheek. She tried to move out the way but with the cast on her arm and my grip, she wasn't going anywhere.

"Lexi." Her brother said and everyone looked. It took all of two minutes for gunfire to erupt and bodies drop. The crazy part is, the bodies dropping were from my crew. How the hell is that shit happening?

"Let her go and I might allow you to walk outta here." Frankie said and there were at least five guns pointed at me. Some of my guys still had their weapons out too.

"Not a chance. The only way I'll let her go is if I can kill her pops right here." I felt Lexi's head move and she was now staring at me.

28

"Why do you want my father?" I tossed my head back laughing. She still had no clue.

"Your pops need to die because he killed mine." She had a lost stare.

"Oh he didn't tell you. Well let me be the one who does." I wrapped my arm around her throat.

"You see when I was young, my pops used to date your real mother, Erica." I heard her gasp and the look on her stepmother's face told me she knew exactly who I was as well.

"Yea they were a couple for a while and for some reason your pops became jealous of their relationship and killed him."

"Who told you that story?" Her stepmother asked.

"Your mother." I pointed to her father and at that very moment, I knew they had no idea we were in contact.

"Rome are you sure my grandmother told you that?" Lexi asked the best she could with my arm still around her neck.

"I'm positive. Isn't this her name and phone number?" I showed it to her and she looked at her father and nodded yes.

"Rome your father was sexually abusing me. My mother was getting high and let it go on for a while."

"BULLSHIT! My pops didn't need to touch a kid." I was beyond mad she was accusing my father of being a pedophile.

"It's true Rome. We have the documentation from the police, photos of the bruises, medical paperwork of the disease he gave her, and the video footage from the mall when he took her away and into a secluded hallway." Her stepmother said and walked towards me.

"I know how connected her pops is so I'm sure it's made up." I felt wetness on my arm and realized Lexi was crying.

"What the fuck you crying for?"

"Because I voluntarily slept with a man whose father molested me as a child." Everyone standing there may have had their weapons out but you could tell they felt bad for her.

"Stop saying that."

"I can't Rome. You don't know how many nightmares I had, counseling sessions I had to go through and the fact no man could get close enough to me because of it. But you. You knew, didn't you? That's why you were on the campus. You wanted to have sex with the woman who had your father killed. Why would you do that?"

"Like I said, my pops didn't do that and I only fucked you to get close to your father. Granted, it took forever but here we are now and I'm about to take him away from you, the same way he took my father away from me." I pointed the gun at him and he lifted his hands up. This nigga had no worry in the world.

"Take your best shot nigga but you better kill me."

"Daddy no!" She cried out.

"I won't miss."

"APRIL NOOOOOO!" Her father shouted.

BOOM! I shot and missed him but caught her stepmother.

That motherfucker dropped to his knees and her brother ran over too. Lexi was fighting to break loose but I held her ass like my life depended on it. Well it did because all the men in there had to meanest look on their faces.

"Yo, let's get the fuck outta here." I walked out backwards and the guys with me did the same.

"LET ME GO!!!!" Lexi screamed and kept tryna to make me let her go. I guess she forgot about the cast but I didn't. Once I got in the driver's side of the truck, I tossed her ass on the ground. She laid there screaming as I sped off.

I heard gunshots hitting the back of my truck and all of a sudden, the tire blew. Cops were flying past us in the direction of the hospital. I refused to stop and called up one of the new guys to pull on side of me so I could jump in the truck they were in. Hell yea, we had one of their men on our side. He despised SJ and its always good to have a scorned employee on your team.

"Yo, when did you get hit?" He asked and pointed to the blood on my leg. I guess with everything going on I didn't feel it.

"No clue. Drive me to a hospital at least an hour away."

"I don't think you're gonna make it."

"JUST DO IT!" I shouted and picked my phone up to dial this bitch. Was she really lying about my father? Did he molest Lexi? My mother never told me the real story of why he was killed. She'd just say he did some shit he had no business and got what he deserved. It sounded harsh every time but if what I heard is true, I see why.

"Hello Rome." She had the nerve to sound aggravated in the phone.

"Did you really send me after your son for killing my father, knowing he molested your granddaughter?" She remained silent for a moment.

"No one knows if it's true or not."

"Why would they lie about something like that?"

"Why not? They would never accept you marrying my granddaughter anyway because of who your father is. They'd make up anything to save face." I sat there tryna decipher who to believe. This woman came in my life outta nowhere asking me to kill her son's wife. Should I listen to anything she has to say?

"How are you?" An older woman said as she approached me in the sneaker store.

"Fine. How are you?" I'm thinking she's just someone in the store who spoke like most people and continued trying on my sneakers.

"Can we talk somewhere?" I glanced around the store to see who she was speaking to and she pointed to me.

"Ugh, let me pay for these and I'll meet you in a few minutes." Instead of her waiting outside the store, she stood right next to me. The employee had to be thinking the same thing; like who the hell is this lady and what does she want.

I paid for my stuff, walked out and over to the bench outside the store. She sat first and started asking me if my father was Glen and did I know how he died. It really made me wonder why she was here. I told her, he was my father and someone murdered him. She asked if I knew who? I told her no and this bitch started telling me all types of shit; like how my pops was in love with this Erica chick and she had a bratty daughter who she loved but couldn't stand at times. Then her son came home, became jealous of Erica's boyfriend, which was my father and killed him. At the time, I had no idea the guy

34

who killed my pops was her son and I still didn't until she asked if I would kill his wife for revenge.

"Who's his wife?" She gave me her name and showed me a photo. The woman was beautiful as hell.

"Look, I don't want you to harm my son unless necessary but I need his wife gone ASAP."

"If I'm gonna kill anyone lady it would be your son because he killed my father. It only makes sense. An eye for an eye." She stood.

"Yes but I'll pay you five hundred thousand dollars to kill her and leave my son alone." My eyes grew big as hell.

"Fine. When you want me to do it?" She kissed my cheek and promised to be in touch.

"Wait! How do I know where to find you?" She smiled.

"You don't. I'll find you but until then, this is the school my granddaughter attends. Get in close with her and she'll lead you straight to them. When it's done, the money is yours."

"Why am I getting close with the daughter?"

"You'll figure it out." She blew me a kiss and was gone in the wind.

From that day on I made it a mission to find this granddaughter of hers and it didn't take long once I got to the school. I had money, not a lot but enough and rented an off-campus apartment and paid a dude who was in the work study program to make me an ID. It gave me access into the buildings so I can pretend to be a student. He even gave me a fake schedule. Money goes a long way when you want something done.

Anyway, I met Lexi and it just so happened that she wasn't speaking to her male best friend and refused to go home. Her family came to visit but I was always away at the time making money. I wasn't really pressed about finding her family yet because I was doing other shit and I had a girl and kids that I couldn't let Lexi find out about. I wasn't ashamed or anything its just I could tell she wasn't into a man with kids at the time. She was very needy and required a lot of attention.

That was three years ago and now I just shot her stepmother who jumped in front of her pops. I should've kept

Lexi with me in order to find him again. It's ok though because I know where they live. I'm sure its gonna be hard to get close to them. Oh well, I have a team behind me and I will get him by any means necessary.

Kane Jr.

"Ma, please get up." I felt the tears falling down my eyes and they began to blur my vision. Blood was pouring out her stomach and her eyes were fluttering. My dad had his hand on her stomach to try and stop the bleeding but nothing was working.

"Oh my God." I heard and turned around. Frankie had Lexi in his arms and her entire body was shaking. Some nurses ran over and had him take her in one of the rooms.

"Sir, let her go so we can help her." I heard the doctor saying to my father.

"Do that shit right here. I need to see you make her better." I have only seen my father cry once and it was when Lexi was shot. Now I'm watching him, watch his wife; my mother; bleed out and he most likely has no idea Lexi is even here. It was so much commotion going on and police were everywhere.

"All the medical equipment is in another room. Sir, we're losing her. Let me help her." The doctor pleaded.

"Come on Kane. You need to check on Lexi." Frankie's pop said. My father stood with my mother in his arms and laid her on the stretcher. The doctor and nurses rushed my mom outta there.

"Where's my daughter?" Cops were walking in and so were detectives. It's like the place became more and more crowded.

"Pops there she is." I pointed to the doctor pushing her in another room. We ran over and my sister was seizing or something. The doctor injected her with a liquid and slowly she began to calm down.

"I need an EKG, an EEG and a MRI for her leg." We both looked down and one of her legs were twisted. They started putting monitors on her chest, the blood pressure cuff and an IV.

"I'm gonna kill her." I followed behind him because I know he meant my grandmother.

"Not right now." Frankie and Dree's father stood in front of us.

"I have to. Do you see what the fuck my mother did? My wife is fighting for her life and my daughter is seizing."

"I know and I can't imagine what you're going through. However, you don't want them to follow you outta here." Arnold said. We both looked and it was so any cops its guaranteed that they would.

"And you need to be here when the doctor comes out. Have you checked on your brother and nephew?" Dree's dad asked and that's when we both remembered they were the reason we came.

"I don't even know if they're alive and right now, I can't go back there." My pops fell back on the chair and used his elbows to lean on his knees. His fists were under his chin and even with the tears falling, I knew he was in deep thought. He had to be tryna figure out a way to kill my grandmother.

"I'll go." My father looked at me.

"I'm the only other family member out here besides aunt Essence and she's in the corner about to pass out again." I pointed and we all looked. Essence was petrified and Dree and her mom were tryna comfort her.

40

"Nah, I'll go."

"It's ok pops. I got it. Stay here and wait for them to tell us about ma and Lexi. Can y'all make sure he don't leave?" I asked Arnold and Dreek.

"We got him. Go see what's going on." I noticed Raya's dad stare at me but I think he knew not to address me again. At least not right now.

"You good?" I asked Frankie who was sitting in my sisters' room crying.

"Yea. I'm waiting for them to bring her back. I'm gonna kill that motherfucker. I'm killing his momma, baby momma, aunts, uncles and anyone else he knows. I swear if I killed kids they'd be dead too."

"You wanna come with me to check on SJ and my uncle?" He wiped his face and stood.

"Shit, with everything going on I forgot."

"We did too. Let's go." I asked the nurse where to identify my relatives and once she asked me their names, she sent me upstairs to ICU. I thought it was weird because when they tell you to identify someone it's usually in the morgue.

I pressed the elevator and noticed the blood on my hands from my mom. I won't even try and begin to understand why she jumped in front of a bullet. My dad and her kids meant everything to her, so I'm mad she did it but I get it. Unfortunately, it's at the expense of her life. That bullet went straight into her stomach.

When her body dropped my world came crumbling down. If you can't tell I'm a mama's boy and seeing her like that broke me. It's one thing to see people you kill die, but when that person is your parent or sibling, it does something to you.

"Let's go in the bathroom to clean up before we see them." We opened the door and went straight to the sink. It wasn't much we could do about our clothes but at least the blood was off our hands and face. I opened the door and pressed the button to get in ICU. The doors opened and everyone stared at us.

"Look. A lotta shit happened downstairs in the emergency room. All I'm here for is to check on my uncle and cousin." No one said a word.

"Anderson is the last name." They still stood there.

"YO WHAT FUCKING ROOM IS MY FAMILY IN!" I shouted and one of the nurses started typing on the computer. Don't ask me why she did that when it ain't that many rooms on the floor.

"They're in rooms 103 and 104."

"Why they in separate rooms?" Frankie asked.

"There's only one bed per room." Neither of us said anything and walked in the first room. My uncle was laying there with an oxygen mask, tubes and monitors all over his chest. His stomach and leg were wrapped up as well. You could tell he was heavily sedated. I left and went in SJ's room and this nigga was up watching television.

"Oh shit nigga. I'm glad to see you're ok." I ran over and hugged him and Frankie did the same.

"Where's my mom and is my pops ok?"

"Your mom is downstairs and your pops is next door." We didn't tell him much because he'd probably flip out.

"How the hell are you in here and awake?"

"They kept me on this floor in case the person who did this tried to come here. Is that blood on y'all? What the fuck happened?" I was about to send his mom a message and tell her SJ is fine and that my uncle is asleep but stopped.

"Code Blue in operating room 5. Code Blue in operating room 5." The woman said on the loud speaker and I took off. I ran to the desk and asked where the operating room is. These bitches were scared as hell but even more scared when I pulled the fucking gun out.

"Ummmm it's the floor below us."

"Good. You." I pointed to some chick.

"Me?" She pointed to herself.

"Yes you." I snatched her by the head and basically drug her around the desk.

"Take me down there. I'm gonna need a card go get in and you have one."

"If any of you bitches think about calling the cops, I promise to murder each and every one of your family members." Frankie barked as he stood by SJ's door. They all put their hands up.

"Please don't kill me." The chick cried.

"Bitch, ain't nobody tryna kill you."

"Then why are you doing this?" She stepped on the elevator with me.

"Because I had a bad fucking day and I need to make sure my mom isn't the one they called a Code Blue on."

"Your mom?"

"Yes my mom. Fuck! And my sister and my girl." I had my hands on my head tryna keep it together because I've been known to lose it. The doors opened and she tried to run off. I grabbed her by the hair.

"Try that shit again and I promise to splatter your brains on this fucking wall." She nodded and used her card to open the doors on the surgery floor.

"Hey girl. What you doing down here?" One of the nurses asked and looked directly at me.

"Listen ma. I'm not in a good mood, and this bitch think I won't kill her. All I wanna know is if my mom, sister and girl are ok."

"Ok. What's the names?" She didn't give me any problems. I gave her the information and waited.

"Ok. Alexis Anderson is down having an MRI. She's fine." I was happy to hear that.

"April Anderson is in surgery and Raya Hollis just came outta surgery."

"I wanna see my mother."

"I can't let you in there." I gave her a look.

"I would if I could but the only people who have that key card are the doctors but I can take you to the window." She gestured with her index finger for me to follow her and I still had this dumb bitch by the arm.

"Was the Code Blue on my mom?"

"Oh no. That was on this patient here?" She let me look in a room and the doctors were removing their scrubs and cleaning up. I felt a relief seeing it wasn't my mother.

"This is the room your mom is in." I looked in that tight ass window and saw the tube hanging out my mom's mouth, her hair had a blue cap on it and people were hovering around her. I turned and slid down the wall.

"I'm staying right here." I had my knees up and let my head rest against the wall.

"You can't stay here." I gave her an evil look.

"I'm not leaving her. What if he comes back to finish the job? I need to protect her. Fuck that? Call the cops. This will be a fucking hostage situation because I'm not moving." Both of the women now had sad faces.

"I'll be right back." She grabbed the idiotic chick who brought me on the floor and walked away.

A few minutes later, I heard a woman's heels coming closer. They stopped in front of me and the person offered me a water. I looked up and the she appeared to be in her late thirties or mid-forties and she wasn't bad looking. She pulled a chair up next to me and sat down.

"How long have you been here?" I shrugged my shoulders.

"Are you ok? Do you need anything?"

"No. I'm just waiting for my mom."

"I understand but it's not protocol for you to be on this floor." I glanced up at her.

"Before you snap, let me explain why." I twisted the cap off the bottle and took a sip.

"The entire hospital is sterile but this floor is a little more sterile if that makes sense. What I mean is, you have to be in scrubs to be here and it's also a distraction to the doctors knowing a family member is actually on the floor and possibly watching them perform."

"Who the fuck cares? At least I'm not in the room."

"Ok but how would your mother feel knowing you did all this to get on the floor? Would she be ok with you pulling a gun out on women or bullying your way here?" I started laughing.

"Nah, she'd kick my ass if she knew."

"That's what I thought. How about I take you to check on the other two women you inquired about and hopefully they'll be word on your mom." She stood and put her hand out to help me up.

"This way." She walked on the side of me and asked me a few questions about what went down. She wasn't surprised to hear I'm with the family from the emergency room.

I asked had she been down there and she told me no because the place was on lockdown. She opened the door to some room and you could hear the monitors. A nurse was checking the machine, pressed a button and stepped out.

"I'll give you a minute." She closed the door. I moved over to Raya and noticed how swollen her face was. She had a black eye, a nose brace on and her there was a cast from her hand all the way up to her shoulder. One of her legs was hanging by something in the air, to keep it elevated. She definitely had a broken leg. I grabbed her other hand.

"Baby, I don't know if you can hear me but I need you to wake up. I'm sorry about the argument we had and if you still wanna wait to tell your dad, I will. Just come back to me. Please don't leave me." I heard the door open and assumed it was the lady.

"I love you Raya and I'll see you soon." I kissed her lips and someone cleared their throat. I turned around and her parents were standing there.

"I'm leaving." I went to leave and her father stopped me.

49

"I don't know who you are and I'm pissed about that video. But I see you love my daughter and when the time is right we need to talk." I nodded and turned to go.

"Can you tell her I was here and I'll be back as soon as I hear about my sister and mother?" Her mom walked up to me.

"They're gonna be fine young man."

"I hope so."

"You have a strong family. Go be with them and Raya will be here."

"Thanks." I stepped out the room and the lady walked me down to the emergency room again. We went in the room where my sister was and she was lying there hugging my dad.

"Is mommy ok?" She asked when she saw me. The woman left and closed the door. My father stood.

"She's still in surgery. I saw her dad and.-"

"And what?" I just broke down at that moment. I tried my hardest to hold it in until I made it home but seeing them, Raya and my mom, I couldn't do it. My father hugged me and had me sit down.

"We're gonna get through this."

"Daddy did you call nana?" That's my mother's mom. She was traveling the country with her doctor husband. They married after I was born.

"I will when they tell me about your mom." He sat next to Lexi on the bed and she laid under his arm. All of us remained in silence letting the television watch us. I pulled my chair closer to the bed and laid my head on the bed. Her leg was fractured and had a brace on it. They still had her in an arm cast and she had monitors on her head to check for seizures. The doctor said, it may have happened from the fall. At least she was ok and so is Raya. All we were waiting for is to hear about my mom.

"Hello Mr. Anderson." A doctor walked in and we all sat up. I prepared myself for the worst but hoped for the best.

Lexi

"Hey baby." Frankie strolled in the room as the doctor was beginning to speak.

After Rome tossed me out the car, I screamed and don't know what happened after that. My brother told me Frankie brought me in shaking and they had to give me some sort of sedative to calm down. Fortunate for me, my leg was only sprained and required one of those knee braces. I had to stay overnight for observation and for them to figure out if I had any seizure activity going on in my head.

"Hey. The doctors about to tell us what's going on with my mom." He stood on the side of the bed.

"Tell me about my wife." My dad was standing in front of him with his arms folded. He still had the same clothes on and they were covered in blood.

"Your wife suffered a gunshot wound to her abdomen, in which the bullet ruptured her spleen and punctured a hole in her lung. We had to give her a full hysterectomy and fix her intestines. Right now, she has a colostomy bag until she can get out of bed to use the bathroom."

"Can we see her?" My father asked.

"Right now she's in recovery but as soon as she's in a room, I'll have someone come get you."

"Thank you." He shook all of our hands and stepped out. Arnold's father walked in with two officers and I gripped my dad's hand. My brother stood and Frankie was next to him.

"I'm sorry to bother you at this critical time but we have to place this young man under arrest." They pointed to my brother.

"WHAT?" I screamed.

"What for?" My dad spoke up.

"He went on the ICU floor, basically held a nurse hostage and forced her to take him on a different floor." My brother smirked.

"Kane Jr. what happened?" He came over to me.

"Fuck that stupid bitch." Frankie yelled out mad.

"I heard Code Blue and had to make sure it wasn't mommy. Then, I needed to check on Raya."

"Raya? What happened to her?" I was confused because not only was my family in here, so was his girlfriend.

"Someone ran a red light and hit her. She flipped a few times but she's ok."

"Oh my God. Why is all this happening?"

"I'm good sis and I don't know." He stood in front of the cops, placed his hands behind his back and I watched them put handcuffs on him.

My family has endured so much in these last few weeks, I don't know how much more we can take. My brother looked at Frankie who nodded and was escorted out. The nod only meant whoever the nurse is, won't make it through the night.

"Stay here with your family. I'll handle it." Frankie's dad said and he and my father shared a hug.

"I owe you big time."

"We good. We'll be related soon so consider us family too." He winked at me and stepped out.

"Daddy, I wanna see mommy." I may be grown but I felt like a baby when it came to my parents.

"You will. Frankie, make sure it's done before this night is over."

"Already on it." He was texting away on his phone.

"Lexi, I need some fresh air. I'll be back." I knew it meant he wanted to smoke. I nodded and laid back in my bed. Frankie scooted next to me.

"I don't know what's going on babe but from now on, I want you staying with your parents."

"Frankie." He put his two fingers up to my lips.

"I'm gonna be there too but our house isn't safe and I'll be damned if you get hurt again."

"Baby, I don't want you getting in trouble. With everything going on and half my family outta commission, I don't know what I'd do if anything happened to you." He smiled.

"You don't have to worry about me. My pops, yours and our team are pretty tough. How you think we laid all those niggas out?"

"But Rome is still out there."

"You must be crazy if you thought any of us would shoot at him while he had you. He knew that too, which is why he kept you in front of him. Sucka ass nigga used you for a shield." His face was turned up as he spoke about what went down in the emergency room.

"I know and I'm sorry I couldn't get away for you to get him." He used his hand to grip my chin.

"Don't ever be sorry for something you had no control of. You have a cast on your arm and still haven't healed from the shot in your side. Nobody expected you to do anything."

"I know but my mom took a bullet for my dad, my brother just got arrested, my cousin and uncle are hurt. I'm scared..." He cut me off and wiped my eyes.

"I'm not saying you shouldn't be but I'm gonna do everything in my power to keep you safe." He kissed my lips and it started becoming too much because his erection was now growing and my body wanted him.

"I want you Lexi."

"I want you too. Close the door." We weren't gonna be able to do much but something is better than nothing. He

56

hopped up but it was too late. My dad was coming in with my aunt, Dree and her parents.

"Ummmm, what were you two about to do?" Dree said with a smirk on her face.

"Nothing heffa. It was loud out there and.-"

"Whatever. Don't lie because your dad in here." I gave her the finger.

"Frankie did Kane Jr. identify them? I called the funeral home." My aunt Essence asked.

"Funeral home? Why would you do that?" He questioned and they all looked at him. When him and my brother came in my room, they told us how SJ and my uncle were doing but must've forgot to tell her.

"The officer said at the house to come..." Frankie went over to her and Dree.

"Both of them are in ICU but SJ's fine. Your husband suffered a lot more and has a lotta machines on him. He's gonna be ok if he makes it through the night." The shocked expression on her face showed and she couldn't believe it.

"WHAT? Why did the cops make it seem like...?"

"They had to Essence. What if the people standing there, were the ones who shot them? The cops didn't know." My dad responded and she nodded.

"I'll be back. Wait! Are you ok Lexi? Have they said anything about April?" I smiled because I saw how happy she was and yet; she still made sure I was good too.

"Go see your husband and son. We'll talk when you come back." I told her.

"You coming Dreeka?" She asked and Dree and her parents left out.

"This has been a crazy few weeks." My dad blew his breath and sat down. Stress was written all over his face.

"You ok?" Frankie questioned and we both stared at him.

"Yea. Just tryna figure out how Ima kill my mother."

"Umm let me go check on SJ and handle that other issue." He pecked my lips and walked out.

"You don't have to dad. We can just stay away from her." I didn't want him to murder his mom but at this point, it may not be such a bad idea.

"I have to and I'ma tell you why." He sat up.

"One... your brother is gonna do it, if he gets to her first."

"Well yea." I couldn't disagree.

"And two... this is only one person she's sent after me. Who's to say she won't do it again? And she put you in it by sending him there to find you."

"You think she did?" Again, I didn't wanna believe my grandmother was that sheisty but everything pointed to it.

"It's the only way he'd be able to get me."

"But she could've told him where you were." He stood up and came to sit with me.

"She could've but it would've been too easy for us to figure out she was behind it. Being it took him this long, none of us would've guessed your grandmother sent him, had he not said it." I listened to him and it all made sense now.

Rome asked me a million times to meet my family and I always found a reason not to. Even when they came to visit, I still never allowed it. Part of me always assumed Frankie would come with them but he never did. Then within the last year he began to disappear more and more. He claimed it was nothing and I can't help to think he's been plotting. And last but not least, he popped up unannounced and gave me some line about seeing my address on mail in my room. It didn't dawn on me that I never received any from home until now.

"What now? He's still out there and we have no idea what happened to SJ or who did it."

"Don't worry Lexi. Everything will reveal itself in due time."

"You think so?"

"Yup! Now once I see your mother's ok myself, I'll handle everything else." I nodded and the two of us laid there waiting for them to take us to my mom. I really hope and pray this is the last bad thing to happen. I'm not sure we can handle more.

Frankie

Man, shit was going from bad to worse in such a short time. I got the woman I wanted, yet; she's been shot and attacked. Her family is suffering a lotta hurt, and to deal with the grandmother from hell is even worse. How can a woman be so evil, she'd try and have her son's wife murdered? I've heard of some evil shit people do within the family but that's crazy.

Now I'm down here at the police station with my pops to get Kane Jr. out. I told Lexi I would check on SJ again but with Dree and his mom going up there, I'm positive he'll be fine. I'll make my way up there when I'm done. Plus, once Kane is released, he and I have some unfinished business to handle.

"Come on Mr. Jones. You know it's gonna be hard to cover up the hospital fiasco." The captain whined as we sat in his office.

"How much?"

"Well it was quite a bit of bodies, scared witnesses and.-" My pops hopped up out the seat and grabbed him by the collar.

"I said, how much?" The captain was scared as hell.

"Ummm, whatever you give is fine." My pops pushed him in the chair. The guy fixed his tie and wiped the sweat beads off his face that appeared outta nowhere. He picked up a sticky note and pen to write something down.

"Is this a good number." I glanced over my pops shoulder and it said 100k.

"Yup!"

"Ok. I guess were done here." We all stood. He radioed in the call to have Kane Jr. brought from the back.

"We're done. The money will be in your account soon." We walked to the door.

"Oh, and someone will be watching to make sure you clean this shit up correctly. There better not be any mistakes." My pops said and left him standing there stuck on stupid.

"Who watching him?" I asked as we went to the front of the building.

"Nobody but he don't know that. I have to make him think it so he doesn't mess up." I nodded.

"100K seems like nothing." I referred to the amount requested.

"Its not. I actually thought he'd go to at least half a mill but I'm good with what he asked for." We both laughed.

The two of us sat there talking about Raya. My aunt and uncle weren't taking it well and even though she came outta surgery, it was still touch and go just like it is with SJ's father. After a good twenty minutes went by, Kane Jr. came out with a smirk on his face. None of us spoke a word on the way out and went straight to the car. I knew what he wanted to do and so did my pops, which is why he drove us where we needed to go. It wasn't far but when you're in a zone and ready to get it over with it feels like forever.

We opened the door, stepped out and walked over to the house. You could hear someone screaming from the outside. You'd think we'd run in but since we know who it is, there's no need. Kane had a hateful look on his face and I couldn't blame him. The way he reacted in the hospital is the exact way

63

I would've, had it been my mother. Shit, if I wasn't able to get to Lexi, I'd be flipping the hell out too.

We stepped inside and the nurse sitting in the chair had blood coming down her nose and tears racing down her face. Of course, I had someone snatch her ass up after hearing she contacted the police and had Kane Arrested. He may have been wrong for the way he handled it but he didn't kill her and she should've been understanding to what he was going through. The rest of the nurses obviously did because when they were asked if Kane did anything to them, they all said no. I guess she wanted to be the tough one and look where it got her.

"Please let me go. I promise to drop the charges." She yelled out and we laughed.

"Its funny how bitches wanna plead their case when they know shit is about to go left."
Kane walked over to one of the guys and picked out what he wanted to use for her. There were all types of weapons of choice and I'd hate to be her. Then again, I'd hate to be anyone who pissed any of us off.

"Please." She continued begging and crying.

64

"I told you at the hospital no one would kill you but you had to be the one to call the cops." Kane was very calm speaking to her.

"I'm sorry." You could tell when Kane picked the machete up, that she used the bathroom on herself.

"Its too late for regrets now." And just like that, her head was detached from her body. It may sound gruesome and the sight is; however, it doesn't pay to be the tough one. I'm sure the other nurses will put two and two together when she doesn't return to work.

"I need to get back to the hospital."

"Me too." I told him and watched as he kept the machete in his hand. We didn't trust anyone and disposed of our own shit. That way we knew if anyone found it, it would be our own fault.

"Let me go home and change first." I nodded and my pops dropped both of us off and went to check on my mom, who left not too long before us. Listening to that fuck nigga say he's the son of the guy who molested Lexi, did something to her.

I'm the product of the same type of nigga but the difference is, I'd never seek revenge on innocent people. Yea, I know my biological father raped quite a few women, one who I know for sure terminated a pregnancy from him. It doesn't make me wanna go find her and ask why? Nor, would I harass any kids he may have out there from a woman or women who did keep a child. Those people did nothing to me, like Lexi did nothing to him. His beef was with big Kane and instead of just coming for him, he went after my woman and that's a no, no. I plan on killing him on sight and would have if he didn't use her as a shield.

Then his dumb ass pointed a gun at big Kane and said he wouldn't miss and did anyway; catching Mrs. April. When I saw her father drop and Kane Jr. run over, I knew then this nigga was a dead man walking. Not that he wasn't anyway after finding out the other shit but almost killing someone's wife and mother, isn't anything I see them letting slide.

Then you have the grandmother who set the entire thing up. I can't for the life of me imagine what big Kane is going through. But I do know he better get to her first because once his son does, ain't no one gonna be able to stop him.

"I'm stopping at the store and I'll be right there." I told Lexi when I answered her call.

"Can you bring me some clothes and I'm hungry for a sub."

"I already got your clothes. Does your dad wanna eat?"

"Daddy, you hungry." I heard her ask in the background. I took their order and told her I'd be up there shortly.

I pulled up at Subway and waited for their subs to be made. I got one for SJ, who had Dree call and ask where I was for the same reason as Lexi. I swear they were definitely twins because they even think alike. I also picked up some stuff for everyone else up there in case they were hungry. You can't go wrong with tuna and turkey subs when you're not sure who eats what. Ain't no pork in either one.

"I haven't seen you in a while." I heard and turned around to see Crystal standing outside her car. How did this bitch know where I was? There's no way she followed me because she had no idea where I stayed.

"What?" I placed all the food in the passenger side of the car and closed the door.

"Nothing." She came closer.

"I miss us Frankie. Why did you up and leave me?" Her hand was on my chest and the other one made its way into my sweats. I can't even front, she was definitely turning me on. I love wearing sweats and I should've been on point knowing bitches will do that shit quick.

"Mmmm, I see you're ready for me."

"Back up Crystal." I pushed her off and opened my car door. I never should've allowed her that close or to get my dick semi hard.

"Don't worry about anything Frankie. No one is out here." She waved her hand around the area. No one was out here but it didn't mean, she'd get anything from me.

"I don't give a fuck if we were in a room. You still ain't getting none." I went to close the door and she grabbed it.

"Come on Frankie. Let me get some one last time." She lifted her shirt to show me she had no bra on. *Did this bitch plan this?*

"I'm good Crystal." I felt myself getting hornier and slammed the door shut. She stood there with a grin on her face. I'm not gonna lie, she could've got it if Lexi wasn't my girl.

I waited a long time to get my woman back and nothing or no one is making me fuck up. Granted, she should've never been close enough to even touch me but at least, I didn't fuck her. *Right?* I'll tell Lexi when she's feeling better. I don't wanna upset her, especially with those monitors on her head.

****

"Mmmmm, baby this sub is so good." Lexi moaned out after biting into her food.

"Where's you dad?"

"They just came in and took him to my mom. Kane Jr. went too."

"Oh shit he beat me here?"

"Yea. We thought he would go see my grandmother but once your dad called and said he was home changing, my dad stayed on the phone with him until he came."

"Damn, he was really gonna take her out." She nodded as she chewed.

"He still wants to but my dad told him it's his job to do it."

"How you feel about it?"

"I don't really. I mean she set all of this up and now my family is laid up in here because of it. We have no idea what happened with SJ yet, so who knows if she set that up too." I totally forgot to ask him what went down. After Kane pulled the nurse off the floor, I had to make sure no one called the cops.

"Come here Frankie." She slid the table with the sub on it over to the side after taking one last drink of her soda.

"What's up babe?" I sat next to her and stared. Even with the cast, leg brace, monitors on her head and a few bruises here and there, she was still the most beautiful person in the world to me.

"I know its been a minute since we had sex, and I'm sure you're horny."

"I'm not worried about that right now."

"You may not be, but I am." She slowly let her leg fall to the floor and asked me to stand in front of her. Once she placed her good hand in my sweats, that was it. My shit bricked up harder than when Crystal did it.

"Shit Lex." She stroked me slow, sped up a little and back to slow again.

"You like this Frankie?"

"I love everything you do for me. Ahhh fuck!" I shouted by accident when her mouth wrapped around my dick. Don't ask me how she was able to do it but I damn sure wasn't about to stop her. She took her time pleasing me and whether we had sex or not afterwards it didn't matter because I knew she was about to take care of me like always.

"Cum for me baby. I need to swallow these babies." She sucked harder, placed her hand on my ass and pulled me closer.

"I'm cumming Lexi. Ahhh shit baby." I had to grab onto the side of the bed to keep from falling. I promise she drained the fuck outta me.

"You ok?" She asked wiping her mouth. I knew she was being smart by the smirk on her face. I had to catch my breath before answering her.

"Whatever." She laughed and pressed the button for the nurse to come help her use the bathroom.

"I need a nap." I pulled my sweats up, climbed in the bed and passed the fuck out. My girl had me down for the count and I don't care who knew.

SJ

"Oh my God, you're ok. My mom screamed when she noticed me coming outta my pops room. I had one of the nurses bring me in to see him. He was hit more than me and unfortunately, they had to place him in a medically induced coma.

"Where are you hit at?" She checked me over and hugged me tight.

"I thought the two of you were dead." She let the tears race down her face.

"I'm ok ma." She kissed me a thousand times as if I were a baby.

"What happened? Did his mother set y'all up? Wait! Why did you leave the house?" She bombarded me with questions and she had every right to. We were sitting outside the house and disappeared without even mentioning it.

"I'll fill you in later. Go be with pops."

"I'll be in your room shortly." She kissed me again on the forehead and the nurse wheeled me back into mine.

"Mr. Anderson, do you need anything else?" Its clear as day this chick was flirting with me. She leaned over to put the break on the wheelchair and I could damn near see straight down her shirt.

"No he doesn't. Get your thirsty ass out my man face." Dree was standing there putting her hair up.

"Who are you?"

"Didn't you just hear me say, my man? Don't play me."

"Its cool Dree." I stood slow and maneuvered my way to the bed, the best I could.

"I'm good nurse." She smiled and switched on her way out.

"SJ, I told you, you're gonna make me catch a case with these ho's." I laughed and patted the seat next to me on the bed.

"I only want you though. Fuck them."

"It better be fuck them." She slid in next to me and asked if I needed anything.

"Just you." She pecked me on the lips and began to tell me everything that went down after they showed up the

74

hospital. Its sad the cops made them believe we were dead but I understood why it was said. What I didn't get, is how my grandmother thought it was ok to come for her own son? I mean who goes outta their way to do some shit like that? I'm sure it boils down to April but that too is a bit much.

I know my uncle and his kids are taking it hard. April is the backbone of their family and always tried to keep the peace, even if it meant speaking to my grandmother, whom she hated and despised. My mom is probably going through it as well. Me and my pops were hit and so was her best friend. I have no idea what happened to make all of this go down at once but I do know, Whitney is as good as dead and whoever she had working with her. I know damn well this wasn't something she did alone.

"What happened to you?" I could see the sadness in her eyes.

"I don't even know. Whitney sent me a text.-" She sucked her teeth.

"It was a picture of her in front of your house."

"My house?" She questioned and sat up.

"Yea."

"Why was she at my house?"

"No idea, which is why I drove over there. My pops came because he said he wasn't allowing me to go alone. When I pulled up something felt off. I tried to leave before anything happened but it was too late."

"She was shooting at you?"

"I don't think so because she came towards the truck once the shooting stopped and had a cocktail in her hand."

"WHAT?"

"She had one of those lighter things you use to light a grill too."

"Oh my God." She covered her mouth.

"She went to throw it but I got my gun out fast enough and shot through the windshield. I can't even tell you if I got her because my ass pulled off. We made it to the hospital and my dad was barely holding in. I'm not sure if they assumed I was alone and he most likely caught all the bullets for me."

"SJ."

"Dree, the bullets were coming from everywhere and had it not been for my pops being in the passenger side, I may not be here."

"SJ, your dad is gonna be fine."

"He was shot in the side a few times, his leg and the side of his chest." I laid my head back on the bed.

"I feel like shit because I'm only hit in the side and my calf."

"But how did your dad get hit so much?"

"I'm guessing the angle they were at only aimed at the passenger side for some reason."

"Its probably because the way my driveway is." I nodded because when you pulled in her driveway there were high bushes on the driver's side. The person probably didn't have a good view and waited on the opposite side.

"Before the doctors took me to the back I was able to tell them who I was and where to send the cops. I get why they approached you two the way they did, but they could've told y'all in the car we weren't dead."

"Its ok babe. As long as you're good."

"I thought we were dead when she came head on with that cocktail."

What's wrong with her?" She wrapped her arm on my stomach and laid her head on my chest.

"I don't know and I don't care. When I see her, she's dead on sight." Neither of us spoke a word after I said that. We were both well aware a war was coming and until we found out who is behind this shit with Whitney, we had to stay alert.

"SJ, I have to tell you something." She stared up at me with a smile on her face.

"What's up?" I placed a kiss on her forehead.

"I'm.-" She was cut off when this bitch walked in. Dree hopped off the bed and I grabbed her back when I noticed her fumbling in her bag.

"I see you didn't die or learn your lesson." Whitney said and stood there smiling.

"Learn my lesson?"

"SJ, you think its ok to treat me like shit and I won't retaliate."

"Bitch ain't nobody treat you like shit. He didn't want you so move the fuck on." Whitney tossed her head back laughing. I was more than pissed she was here and I had no gun on me.

"Give us a minute Dree." She snapped her neck like the damn exorcist.

"HELL NO!"

"Dree, go check on my cousin and come right back. Don't touch her on the way out." I whispered in her ear.

"SJ?"

"Do it Dree." She folded her arms and stormed out the room. I don't know what Whitney had in store for me but I couldn't risk her hurting Dree. Its me she wants.

"What's up Whitney?" I moved the covers off my leg.

"You know none of this would've happened if you didn't play with my heart." I tossed my head back laughing.

"Whitney you weren't in love with me." I stood and held onto the wall.

"How can you say that?" I moved closer.

"Because if you were, you'd never allow me to step out with other bitches. You'd never be ok with just being wifey? You didn't care if I disrespected you or not and the fact you tried to kill me and working with someone who is, shows me this has nothing to do with love." I let my hand go behind her head and tilted it back as if I were going to kiss her.

"Don't tell me how I feel. Women tolerate what they want, but it doesn't make their feelings less relevant. I may have had an idea you were stepping out but until you confirmed it, I couldn't be sure.

"The crazy part is, you showing up to Dreeka's house."

"So you shouldn't have been fucking her while we were still together."

"This is why we couldn't be together."

"Why is that?"

"You're so fucking stupid."

"Stupid?" She questioned with her hand on her hip.

"Yea stupid. Had you done your research, you'd know she and I didn't hook up until after I told you it was over." I could see shock on her face.

80

"Everyone knew about you and I and not once did I allow a bitch to approach you, come to your house or even try to kill you. And trust me with that mouth you've got, it's a few who wanted to get at you." She sucked her teeth.

"SJ, you're too close." She finally said when she felt my breath on her skin.

"Because I want you to hear me." One of my hands were around her throat.

"I'm not in the right frame of mind right now but know that I'm going to kill you." She tried to move my hand and I used the other one to squeeze harder.

"You should've left well enough alone but you and whoever you working with, put me and my father in the hospital and the only way to repay you is to take your life."

"SJ." She barely got out. I could see her eyes bulging and her face turning blue, only made her dying better. I was gonna wait but fuck it, she's here now. My strength wasn't where its usually at but it was getting the job done.

"SJ, let her go." I heard and squeezed tighter.

"SJ please. I can't raise this baby alone." Dree said and I dropped Whitney. She was gasping for air and tryna move away from me.

"You pregnant?" She smiled and shook her head yes.

"That's why your greedy ass ate all that food." I thought about her order at McDonalds. It didn't even dawn on me that she could be carrying my seed.

"SJ, I don't want you in jail and she's gonna put you there." I grabbed her close.

"I'm not leaving you or my baby. Shit, you just made me the happiest man on the planet."

"Too bad, she won't live to keep it."

Zzzzzzz. Zzzzzzz. This bitch tased the fuck outta Dree. I caught her before she hit the floor and damn near fell too. My body was weak as fuck and all I wanted to do was go after Whitney. Unfortunately, I had to get Dree checked out. If Whitney made her lose my kid, I promise her death to be ten times worse.

"YO! LET ME GET SOME HELP IN HERE?" I shouted and the same nurse Dree told off came in.

"I see she got smart with someone else huh?"

"WHAT?" I hit that bitch so hard she fell against the wall and was sleep. The other nurses shook their head and assisted me with Dree.

"She always in some shit." One of them said.

"Take that bitch off my chart."

"Is she ok?" The doctor came in looking at Dree. She glanced at the nurse on the floor and didn't even bother to ask.

"The other bitch tased her. Please hurry up and check her. She's pregnant." They had someone bring a stretcher in and placed Dree on it. I made the attempt to go with them but the nurse stopped me.

"Sir, you're bleeding. Let me help you and then take you to her." She opened the bandage and it was bleeding. The stitches weren't busted but blood definitely seeped through. The only thing on my mind at the moment is Dree, my seed and killing Whitney. I had to get the fuck outta here and that's exactly what I'm gonna do.

I told the nurse to get my discharge papers ready and walked to my father's room. There were two big buff dudes at the door, who I'm sure my uncle sent to protect him. They may not be speaking but my uncle ain't grimy to leave my dad unattended. My mom was laying in the bed with him.

"SJ, what's going on?" I told her what happened and she wanted to sign my father out too. I told her it wasn't a good idea and that no one will be allowed on this floor unless its our family and other patient family members, will have to be on a list. I don't care how mad they got. My father's life was in danger as well as mine, and I'm not letting anyone take him away.

"Stay at the house. I don't want you going to Dreeka's and the crazy bitch show up again." I promised to stay there but knowing Dree's parents, they'll want her to stay there and I'm good with that because I expect to be out looking for Whitney and whoever shot us.

After the nurse brought me the discharge papers, I signed them and waited for someone to fill me in on Dree. In the meantime, I contacted her folks and told them to come back to the hospital. Once they saw I was ok earlier, they wished me

better health and left. Their other kids were home driving the
nanny crazy.

I don't know what's going on but its about to be some
shit. I hope my uncle put the captain on alert. Because I'm not
stopping until everyone who's fucked with my family is six
feet below, including my grandmother.

Dree

"Where's my son? Is my baby ok?" I shouted when I woke up. My parents were looking at me like I was crazy and I didn't see SJ anywhere.

"You're fine Dree." My dad said and brought my son over to me.

"You know I'm gonna kill that bitch." My mom said and walked over.

"Can you believe she did that? I'm the one who stopped SJ from killing her stupid ass." I shook my head and kissed my son on the forehead.

"Why was he gonna kill her anyway?" My dad asked and after I told them what went down they both were annoyed.

"Dree." I put my hand up before my mom could even say it.

"Ma, daddy was the same type of person."

"I didn't even say anything."

"I know but you're thinking it. SJ has a lotta baggage right now and you don't want me caught up in it and trust me I don't wanna be."

"Then why are you?"

"Because I love him and crazy as it sounds, we fit well together." She didn't say anything because her and my father were like oil and milk too.

"Look honey." She sat on the side of me.

"All I'm saying is be careful. If this chick is coming after you over him, then she's not gonna stop."

"I know and I trust him to handle it because he knows, I'm not going to stick around for no drama. I didn't with Herb and I'm not about to with him."

"That's good to know but you have a son and a baby in your stomach to worry about now. Make sure you take every precaution to be safe." She kissed my cheek and my son reached out for her.

"Nana, I want juice." She sucked her teeth because my father dug in the bag and got it for him. They always said the other spoiled him too much when they're both bad.

87

"When can you I go home?" I asked and glanced at the monitor on the side of the bed. I saw the zig zag lines with my baby's heartbeat on it and smiled. I wasn't ready for another child but I also knew the consequences of having unprotected sex.

"The doctor said when you get up, ring the bell and as long as you're ready, you can go. Oh, and SJ said he'll be back and if you leave before then to call him."

"Where did he go?"

"I have no idea but he waited for us to get here first." My dad said and took my son from my mother.

"Ok." I pressed the button for a nurse so I can leave and an hour later, I was being pushed in a wheelchair to the main lobby.

On the way down, my son kept us laughing with some of the questions he asked about the people he saw. My dad thought it was the funniest shit ever. I guess he would being he lets my son do and say whatever he wants around him. He can do no wrong and no one can discipline him unless he says so, which is why I keep his ass home when he in trouble.

Of course, after one day of not seeing him my father is at the house wondering why. I guess he won't have to worry now because SJ told them not to let me go home. He doesn't know what Whitney did when she was there and he didn't feel it was safe.

We stopped at the Chinese restaurant on the way to grab some food for dinner. It seemed like everyone was there and they too, asked me a bunch of questions. I gave them the shortest answers possible, grabbed me a plate and went to my room. My brother had lil man, and he was in his glory because my brother promised he could play the game with him. I sat down to eat and my phone went off. I looked at the message from SJ and smiled.

SJ: *Can you stop by and see me?*

Me: *For?*

SJ: *Come see.* He left a smiley face emoji after the text and told me to meet him at his parents.

After I ate, I showered and told my parents I'd be back. They didn't even bother to ask where I was going. I'm sure they knew it was to see SJ. My father did tell me to call or send a text when I got to wherever I was going.

Walking to the car did make me a tad bit paranoid so I made sure to check my surroundings before getting in. I started the car and drove to SJ's parents house. I called and told him I'm outside and the door opened. I swear this man was sexy as hell and could make me horny just by looking at him. He gestured with his finger for me to come inside.

"Why did you leave the hospital?" I asked as he closed the door.

"I had some things to handle. Plus, I went to check on Lexi and my aunt." He took my hand in his and led me to his old bedroom. You could tell he hasn't been here by how clean it was. I'm not saying he's messy but his bedroom at his house had sneakers lined up, clothes still in bags and shit like that.

"Oh ok." He shut the bedroom door, lifted my shirt over my head and smiled.

"My sperm wasn't playing huh?" I sucked my teeth.

"I'm happy you're gonna have my kid Dree." He gently kissed my lips and sucked on the bottom one.

90

"My woman sexy as hell." He removed my jeans and had me standing there in just my bra and panties.

"And you know how much I love this ass." His hands palmed it and once he squeezed it, I let out a soft moan.

"Look what you did." He pointed to his hard on.

"Well since you're a little incapacitated, let me do some things for you." I squatted and came face to face with his dick.

"Yea Dree." He placed his hand on my head and held on to the dresser with the other.

"Fuck! I'm about to cum already." He yelled and not too long after, I felt his cum hitting the back of my throat.

"You do know I'm gonna wanna eat that." He stood me up and slid his hands in my panties.

"Wet, just the way I like it. Come here." He led me to the bed and I took a look at his body. He still had bandages on his side and calf. I helped him on the bed and he scooted back.

"I can't bend too much so sit on my face."

"SJ, we don't have to."

"Dree, if you don't put your pussy on my face right now, I'm gonna say fuck these stitches and fuck you so hard

91

you can't walk." I busted out laughing and felt a hard smack on my leg.

"Well since you put it that way, I guess I better do it." I took the rest of my things off and climbed on top carefully. His mouth latched on to my clit and a bitch was in fucking heaven. I moaned so loud he had to tell me to be quiet a few times but I couldn't. His tongue game was lethal and I couldn't get enough.

"Fuck SJ. This dick is so damn good." I had my hands on his chest as I rocked back and forth on his dick.

"And so is this pussy. Why the fuck did I wait so long to dig in these guts."

"I'm gonna cum SJ. Shit, baby. Oh my gawdddddd." My body began to shake and he sat up slowly.

"Wet my dick up Dree." He whispered in my ear and my juices ejected outta my body and slid down his.

"Just like that. Now I'm about to get mine." He had me face him and both of us attacked each other's mouth like we've never kissed before. I could feel his dick twitching inside and his fingers were once again on my clit. The harder my nub got, the harder he thrusted under me. I tried to get him to stop because of his stitches but he refused. He hit me with a stroke so hard from the bottom, I almost jumped off. It was painful and pleasurable at the same time.

"Shit Dree. Got damn this pussy good." He bit down gently on my chest, and both of us surrendered to the powerful orgasms and collapsed on the bed. Sex with him is never boring and always put us to sleep. I went in the bathroom, grabbed a rag to clean us both up, put it in the laundry basket and cuddled up next to him.

"I love you Dree and I'm gonna get her and the niggas who shot me."

"I love you too SJ and I trust you to handle it. All I ask is you try and wait until you're better."

"I'll try but I can't make promises if they come after me first."

"I know baby." I laid my head on his chest and fell asleep. I hope whoever is after him waits until he gets well but with enemies, you never know when they'll strike.

****

"So you really with my boss?" I heard Herb behind me as I came out the store.

"Herb, what do you want?"

"I wanna know why you fucking him and couldn't make it work with me? What the fuck he got, that I don't besides money? Huh Dree?" He had me pinned up against the car.

"First off…" I pushed him off me but he remained in my face.

"Don't put your fucking hands on me. You remember what happened the last time." I smirked and pissed him off.

"Oh when he put me in ICU."

"You should be happy that's all he did."

"Why is that?"

"Because he wanted to kill your punk ass but guess who stopped him?" He didn't say anything.

"I did. Your sons mother and you know why?" Again, he stood there silent.

"Because even though you're a bitch ass nigga, my son; you know the one you barely see, loves you and I didn't want him to grow up without you."

"So what you fucked him good or something?" I had to laugh at how ignorant he sounded.

"Whether I did or not should never be your concern. What you need to be worried about is your son and not who I'm opening my legs to."

"But my boss Dree? Do you know how that makes me look?"

"Herb, I don't care about these fucking streets or the people in them. You had your chance with me and all you did was talk big shit and when it came down to protecting me, you turned into a little boy. I could never be with someone who can't protect his family. I could see you being scared of SJ because of who he is but you were scared of everyone."

"Fuck you Dree."

"How you mad at me for calling you out? This the shit I'm talking about." I turned to get in my car when some chick called his name. She came towards us with two kids in her hand.

"Who's that Herb?" Not that I cared but he seemed extremely nervous.

"Go head Dree. We'll talk another time."

"Herb who the fuck is this?" The chick appeared to be mad. I folded my arms and waited for him to check her but as usual, he punked out and tried to push her away.

"Hold on Herb. Are these your kids?" The woman turned back around and it was like a smack in the face. One of the kids looked to be the same age as my son and had a resemblance like a motherfucker.

"Yes, they are and who are you?"

"Herb tell me this little boy isn't the same age as my son." He ran his hand down his face.

"Oh, so you're Dreeka." It was funny how she knew exactly who I was and I had no idea about her.

"Yes and how do you know who I am?"

"If you're asking questions about my four-year-old, then I can only assume you're her." It was like the wind was knocked outta me when she said her kid is the same age as mine.

"Herb you cheated on me and kept her and this child a secret all these years?"

"Cheated? A secret? Honey, we've been together for the last five years and we're married." And just like that I started whopping his ass in the parking lot. My punches were landing on his face and anywhere else they could connect.

"What the fuck you doing?" SJ grabbed me and pushed me away. Where the hell did he come from? I noticed Lexi and Frankie with him.

"He's married SJ." I felt the tears running down my face.

"Dree calm the hell down. Who cares if he's married?"

"SJ, he's been married for God knows how long. My son is only four and those are his other kids." They all looked at the chick who had a weird facial expression as well.

"SJ, you mess with her?" The chick asked and we all snapped our neck, even Herb.

"Melody, don't start no shit." He responded and we were all shocked except Frankie, which I didn't expect him to be. That's his best friend so if something was or is going on between the, he knew.

"Melody? Oh, you two know each other?" This day kept getting better.

"We'll talk at the house."

"Hell no! I need to know right now what the fuck is going on? He's married, with two kids; one who's the same age as mine and the bitch knows you too. Somebody better tell me something." SJ didn't know what to say but that bitch sure did.

"Oh honey, SJ and I were together before me and Herb. He broke my heart when he cheated on me, which is why I moved on."

"What the fuck Melody? You never told me about him." Herb was aggravated.

"Herb, I don't ask about your past and I don't expect to tell you about mine. They're the past for a reason. Except the past came back around not too long ago." I knew something bad was about to be said just by her tone.

"What does she mean SJ?" I felt myself getting angry all over again.

"When I found out about the other kids Herb fathered."

"Other kids?" I was confused.

"Oh yea honey. He has two more. One is two years old and the other one, she had a few months ago." I couldn't believe this punk had multiple kids and didn't tell me.

"Anyway, it just so happened that I ran into SJ. What was that a couple months ago." I pushed SJ off me and Lexi came over to.

"Oh, we definitely rekindled the romance." She smiled.

"Bye Melody. Don't believe that shit Dree."

"What's a couple of months ago?" I asked because people say that and it was really longer than that. I prayed it was.

"Ummm, Herb when did that bitch approach me about her daughter? It was right after you told me some chick he messed with burned his house down." At that very moment I knew when she spoke of. I could be mad but I broke up with him but did he have to sleep with her?

"Dree let me explain. It didn't happen the way she's making it out."

"It doesn't even matter SJ because I broke up with you but why did you lie and say you weren't with another woman?"

"That's what he does best sweetie." She smirked.

"I wouldn't get too attached because once he realizes he has you, that's when he'll start cheating. Its what he did with me and from what I hear, the crazy chick too. Be careful." She stormed off with Herb behind her asking a million questions.

"I'm gone." I slammed the car door and drove off with Lexi on the passenger side. I had no idea she even jumped in.

"Go to my parents' house." I drove there and hid my car in the garage. They had three of them and I never parked inside so he wouldn't even think to look. I went to her room and laid down. How can my life be perfect one minute and shitty the next?

Kane Jr.

"Kane." My mom spoke softly. It's been a week since the shooting and today is the first day she woke up. They didn't have her in a coma but every time she opened her eyes, the pain would be so bad she'd press the morphine button to dispense and be asleep again. Hopefully, this time won't be the same and we'll actually be able to have a conversation with her.

"I'm right here baby." My dad walked over to her. He has been here every day and the only time he left, was to get some fresh air and have a smoke. He would only do it if I were here or SJ and Frankie.

"Can you get me some water?" He poured her a cup and assisted her in sitting up. You could see she was still in an extensive amount of pain from her facial expressions.

"Where are my babies? Is Lexi ok? Where's Kane Jr.?"

"We're right here ma." Lexi and I both stood and went over to hug her. We were extra careful not to do it too tight but it was hard being we missed her.

"Are you ok? Where are your sisters and brothers?"

"It's late ma and the nanny is at the house. They've been here everyday." She nodded slowly.

"How long has it been?"

"A week."

"A week?" She questioned and we all stood there staring at her. It's like the little words she spoke were enough to make us believe she'll be ok but we had no clue.

"You probably don't remember but the pain had you dispensing morphine each time you opened your eyes. It made you fall back to sleep." My dad told her.

"I'm sorry Kane. I couldn't let him shoot you or my babies."

"April, it's ok. But don't ever take a bullet for me again."

"Kane, I'll take one for you and my kids any day."

"Don't say that. I'd rather be the one here and you taking care of the family. April, I lost my mind when you were shot. Then Lexi got hurt again and my son went to jail. They need their mom and so do I." He kissed her and she wrapped her arms around his neck.

"I need all of you too. I wasn't thinking and..."

"It's over now and we have to get you better." My father ran his hand down her face. I really think he'd go crazy if anything happened to her or any of us for that matter.

"I'm sorry Lexi and Kane Jr. I never want you to see any of us in pain and... and..." she tried to talk and my dad shushed her with his two fingers.

"Let's not think about it." He reached over to press the button for the nurse. Once she came in and saw my mom was awake she went to page the doctor.

"Why were you in jail?" Lexi and I started telling her everything when the doctor stepped in. He asked all of us to step out so he could remove the catheter and run a few tests. Of course, my father refused and stayed right there. I didn't blame him because I'd probably do the same.

"How's Raya?" Lexi asked sitting on one of the chairs in the hallway.

"I don't know. I'm about to go there now. You wanna come?"

"No. If it's the first time you're seeing her, I'll give you alone time. Tell her I hope she feels better."

"I will and tell ma, I'll be back in a few." I walked down the hall and told Lexi not to move from in front of the door. I know she's the oldest but ain't no telling if anyone's watching her. I told her I'd stay until she went back in but she pushed me away.

I took the stairs down to the fourth floor and went straight to the nurse's desk. I asked where Raya's room is and one of them pointed and said she had a visitor. I assumed it was one of her parents and waited outside the door. When it opened, some guy stepped out and stared at me. I swore he had an attitude but why, when neither of us ever met? His face wasn't familiar and it seemed like he had on a fake mustache and beard. Call me crazy but its what it looked like. I made my way in Raya's room and her face lit up.

She still had some bruises on her, and the cast on her leg and arm were still there. Her hair was messy and it looked as if she recently woke up. But how could that be when dude just left? I sat on the side of her and stared. We may be young but I could see myself growing old with her. My father always said, you'll know when she's the one because she'll take over your thoughts, mind, and heart. Raya for sure does that with me.

"Who is the guy that walked outta here?"

"Huh?" She seemed confused.

"The guy who just left. Who is he?"

"Kane, I literally opened my eyes when you came through the door. No one was in here." I didn't wanna scare her and left the conversation alone. I excused myself and went back to the nurse's station.

"The guy that just left; where did he go?" Both nurses shrugged their shoulders.

"Do you have a sign in sheet?" I don't know why I asked that when I didn't sign in.

"You know what? Never mind. Call her parents and tell them to get here ASAP. Raya is in danger." Both of them looked at me.

"DO IT!" One of the chicks jumped and started typing on the computer.

"If that guy returns, do not let him in her room."

"But he said he was her uncle."

"Nah, he ain't no kin to her. Matter of fact, I'll be here until her father comes." I heard the chick speaking on the phone. She passed it to me.

"Hello."

"Who is this and why are you visiting my daughter?"

"Mr. Hollis, this is Kane Jr. I came to see Raya now that my mother finally woke up and some guy was leaving her room. When I asked who it was, Raya had no idea anyone was in there because she just woke up."

"WHATTTTTTTT?" I could hear the anger in his voice.

"Can you stay there until I come?"

"You don't even have to ask."

"Thanks." He said and disconnected the call. I hung up and reminded the two women to inform me if the guy returns. I went in the room with Raya and she was tryna get out the bed.

"Hold on." I ran and picked her up.

"I need to use the bathroom." She said with her head down.

"Why you looking down?"

"Because I just woke up and have morning breath." I couldn't help but laugh. I pulled the chain after sitting her on the toilet and waited for the nurse to come. I stepped out and let her help Raya.

As I waited, I began checking the room and something told me to check her purse and phone since it was sitting out. Sure enough, there was a damn tracker inside her pocketbook. I checked in the vent of the heater above the bed and there was another one of those cameras. I ran in the bathroom and Raya didn't have a shirt on. I snatched a towel and placed it over her.

"What's wrong?"

"Raya, I think whoever taped us at your apartment was here. Fuck!" I checked everywhere in the bathroom and was pissed when I noticed it hanging out the vent in the ceiling.

"I'm gonna kill that motherfucker. Hurry up and get her cleaned up." I took the camera out and stomped on it. Who in the hell is watching her?

After about twenty minutes, the nurse and Raya came out and I could see nervousness on both their faces. Not sure why the nurse is scared but I know why my girl is. We helped Raya sit and I bent down to put her sneakers on. Ain't no way in hell she's staying here any longer.

"Raya are you ok?" Her mom ran in just as I stood up.

"Let me talk to you." I followed her pops in the hallway and explained what happened and the shit I found.

"Are you aware of what's on the video that was sent to me?"

"No but when you approached me in the ER, I figured it was bad."

"Bad ain't the word."

"What was on it?" I could assume so many things but I didn't wanna make it seem like I knew anything.

"Let's just say, there's never a time when a father wants to witness his daughter in any sexual acts."

"Say what?" Now I was pissed because I'm her first so who was he talking about.

"I got a video with the two of you having sex."

109

"Who the hell sent you that?" My face was turned up because she and I did some freaky ass shit to one another. I know its not from her being at my house so it had to be from her place at school. I was already pissed someone taped us but to know the person sent it to her pops, is definitely a violation.

"I'm guessing whoever left and put these other cameras in her room." I started pacing and he made a call on his phone telling someone he needed to retrieve the security footage from here.

"I can take her to my house if you want." He gave me the side-eye.

"No disrespect but you already know what it is because you saw the video."

"Thanks, but no thanks. Not saying you can't protect her because it's obvious you're doing a lot. Her mother and I want her home. Plus, you've been back and forth to check on your mom and uncle. She'd be left alone in your house and I'm not comfortable with that right now."

"I respect that but how you know what I'm doing?"

"When you have kids of your own twenty years from now." He smirked. I guess it's his way of telling me not to get his daughter pregnant.

"You'll know everything there's is to know about who's dating them."

"Well can I come by and see her?"

"Absolutely. I'm not as strict as Raya may have made it seem. She is my first born and I don't want her sidetracked due to a man."

"I understand and trust me when I say, I told her to tell you many times."

"I know. Raya has always been afraid to disappoint me and her mother. I don't know why because we've never expected any of our kids to be perfect. However, she's also afraid of falling in love and the relationship doesn't work out. She's very loyal to a fault but you can't help who you fall for." He said and patted me on the shoulder. We walked in and the nurse now had her in the wheelchair. Her mom handed the bags to her father.

"Can we have a minute?" I asked and they stepped out.

"I'll be over when I'm done checking on my mom."

"Kane I'm sorry for not telling him. Maybe if I did, we wouldn't have been arguing and I..."

"Don't blame yourself for anything that happened. It's on me. I left you upset at the house. I should've waited until you calmed down. I'm so fucked up over it and I promise to make it up to you."

"I love you so much Kane but don't blame yourself. I was acting like a spoiled brat. All you wanted me to do is tell my father and I started a fight just so I didn't have to. Baby I'm so, so sorry." She pulled my face close to hers and slid her tongue in my mouth.

"Mmmm." She pulled away and wiped the lip-gloss off my lips.

"I missed you Kane."

"I missed you too."

"You weren't here when I woke up. I thought you didn't love me anymore." I wiped the few tears that came down her face.

"My love ain't going nowhere. Now go with your parents and I promise to stop by. If it gets too late, I'll call you." I kissed her again and pushed the wheelchair out the door. I walked with them to the elevator and once the door shut, went back to see my mom.

"Hey son. Is Raya ok?" My mother asked when I walked in. Lexi was in the bed with her and my dad was lying on the couch.

"Yea she good." I closed the door and moved over to the bed.

"How are you? Move, Lexi damn." I lifted her out the bed and sat her next to my dad. My sister is short and thin so moving her is nothing.

"Daddy why?-"

"It's his turn Lexi." I stuck my finger up at her.

"I'm ok now that I know my family is." I took my sneakers off and got in with her. She stared at me and ran her hand down my face.

"I'll be glad when she goes home. I can't even lay with my own wife because her spoiled ass kids fighting over whose turn it is." We all started laughing because he was big mad.

My mom promised to do some inappropriate things for him when she got better and his attitude changed quick. Lexi told them she was gonna throw up and I second the motion.

"I love you son."

"I love you too ma." I ended up dosing off and even though the bed was tight. It felt like the best sleep ever.

Raya

"Are you sure you're ok?" My mom asked before she left the bedroom. They had been checking on me nonstop since we got here and that's been a few hours. I had a broken leg; my forearm was fractured and there were a lotta bruises. They thought my nose was broken but it wasn't. Thank goodness because I refused to walk around with that thing on my face.

When I first woke up, my parents were sitting there looking stressful as hell. My mom had her head on my dad's shoulder and my siblings were there too. Ray Jr. saw me first and ran over. He was a year younger than me and my best friend. I guess since we were so close in age it made sense but he was super protective over me too sometimes and it got on my nerves. He is the only one in my family who knew about Kane Jr. and that's because they played basketball together in high school.

Kane was the starting point guard and my brother was a forward. He was a sophomore on the varsity team and had become the star player alongside Kane. Both of them were

115

offered hella scholarships but Kane didn't wanna go to school for sports. My brother on the other hand is a senior now and had a ton of choices to choose from.

The NBA scouts had even attended a few of his games but my mom said he had to finish college and she didn't care if it were online or at a campus but he was doing it. She said too many athletes go in the NBA, something happens and they don't have anything to fall back on. Money or not, she never wanted her kids to be dependent on someone else, which is exactly why I wanted to live on my own. My parents were footing the bill but at least I was able to experience that part early.

"I'm good." I smiled and placed the pillow under my foot to keep it elevated. She kissed my cheek and headed for the door.

"Hey, let me talk to you for a minute." My dad said and walked in. So much for me going to bed.

I thought Kane was gonna come over but his sister sent me a picture of him asleep in that tight ass hospital bed with his mom. I may be a daddy's girl but he for sure is a mama's boy. Its cute though because at least I know he will cherish his woman and family the same.

"Do you have any enemies?" I looked at him. He came and sat on the bed next to me.

"Not that I know of. Why do you ask?"

"Because I'm tryna figure out who would send a video like that to me or even tape you for that matter."

"What video?" I was praying he wasn't speaking of the one I got on the way to their house that night. I remember opening the text and a video of Kane and I popped up. It showed Kane having my legs on his shoulders and I couldn't tell you what else because I crashed.

"Someone sent me a video of you and your boyfriend. I don't even wanna discuss what was on it." He had his face turned up, which verified what I knew. I covered my face with both hands and laid back on the bed.

"I'm not upset because you're grown but I don't know why someone would tape you. How the fuck did they even get in your apartment?" He spoke angrily, and I didn't blame him.

He did a massive sweep of my apartment before I moved in and the day of. Then he hired two bodyguards to keep an eye on me. One in the morning and one at night. Granted, they stayed in a different apartment but were always around if I needed them. Now that I think of it, where were they when someone was following me? I can't blame them for someone being in my house because even though they walked me up to my floor and checked the apartment each time, they never thought to check for cameras or anything.

"Daddy the night I called and told you someone broke in my apartment, I left out the part where I was being followed."

"WHAT?" He stood and started pacing. I don't know why I only told him the bare minimum when I should've mentioned everything.

"Where was Michael and Javier?"

"I don't know dad." It was Michael's turn to watch me and I called to let him know my class was cancelled. He said, he was on the way but I left before he could get there.

"I called Kane and he had me pull into the police station. I did get the license plate number." I could see aggravation all over his face. He tried very hard to keep me safe and something still happened.

"Where is the plate number?"

"I gave it to Kane." He nodded and came over to me.

"Raya don't ever hold shit like that in again. I'm not saying Kane won't protect you because he's already shown he will. But you can't hold things in thinking I'm gonna be upset."

"But…"

"But nothing. I may be upset hearing someone was following you, but it won't make me angry with you. Look." He sat down next to me.

"I know you're eighteen and feel like as an adult you don't have to mention certain things but its not the case. With so many lunatics and maniacs out there, you can never be too sure what someone will do." I nodded and he stood to kiss my forehead.

"Give me Kane's number so I can get the plates and see what I can find." I read it off to him without picking my phone up.

"You must really like him if you know his number off hand."

"No daddy. I love him. Matter of fact, I'm in love with him and I'm sorry for not mentioning it sooner. I was scared you'd pull me outta school and blame him as a distraction."

"I knew it was someone but not who. As long as you stay focused on your goal, I don't have any complaints." He closed the door and I slid down further on my bed.

Now that my parents know everything its like a weight has been lifted. Unfortunately, I still have no idea who's following and taping me. At least if I'm home I don't have to worry and I know Kane ain't taping us.

****

"You good?" Kane asked when he helped me in his house. I hadn't seen him in a week because he wanted to make sure his mom was good. I did speak, text and facetime with him every day though.

120

"I'm ok." He lifted me out the wheelchair and sat me on his couch. I couldn't use my arms to walk with crutches and the only way to move around is in a chair. I hated it but him and my parents fought with my ass to stay in it.

"You hungry?" He locked the door and came over to where I was.

"For you I am." He blushed and it was cute. I wasn't lying though. Ever since we had sex, I was hooked and the sad part is we couldn't do anything.

"Soon as you get either the arm cast removed or the leg one, your man got you." He leaned over and kissed me deeply.

"Kane you're not gonna cheat on me because we can't have sex, are you?"

"Make this your last time asking and because this is my last time answering." He lifted my leg on his lap.

"You are my woman. The one, I can't wait to speak to in the morning when I wake up and the one I dream about. There's no one out there I want in my life, or in my bed besides you." Now it was my turn to blush.

"No, you can't give me sex but the fact you're alive after that horrific accident is all I'm worried about right now." I had the biggest grin on my face but his next comment knocked it right off my face.

"And just so you know, I won't take it easy on your pussy when you can have sex again."

"KANE!"

"Kane my ass. You know I don't play that texting and driving shit. You were already upset and should've checked it when you stopped." He kissed me again but this time it was a peck because his phone rang. I could tell it was his mom or sister because of the conversation.

Once he hung up, he ordered us some food. It didn't take long to get there and before we could eat, he checked the bag and all he contents for cameras or listening devices. I was laughing but I understood why he did it. We still had no idea who the person is and the plates they traced from the person following me, were linked to a dead man's identity so we couldn't find whoever it was.

I must say, seeing him this overprotective of me and catering to my needs, only established his spot in my life permanently. I hope he felt the same because I damn sure wasn't letting him go.

Lexi

"Have you spoken to him?" I asked Dree while we sat at my doctor's appointment to get this stupid cast removed. Over the last two weeks all I wanted to do was have this thing taken off so I could sex my man all day and night. I took the leg brace off a week later. My shit was fine.

"Not really. He'll send a text to see if I'm hungry or need anything." I stared at her about to cry again. I swear any mention of my cousin would have her eyes watery and the crying is just as bad.

"Did you address the situation with Melody, who by the way I had no idea about?"

"He tried the first few days but after me not responding to meeting up, he stopped. I wanna believe he didn't have sex with her but I can't. And the fact I broke it off with him only made it fair game."

"What you mean?"

"It means, I can't even get mad. I mean, I can about him saying he wasn't with anyone but in reality, he didn't have to tell me shit."

"I get it Dree but let him explain what really happened. It could be something small." I told her as the doctor walked in.

"Like what? She sucked his dick or something?" The doctor's head snapped and I just shook mine.

"We'll finish this conversation later. Hello, Dr. Ohr. Can we please take this off?" He placed the clipboard on the counter, grabbed some gloves and came over.

"Ms. Anderson, your x-rays came back good and the bone healed quite nicely. I'm going to remove it but I need you to remember that its going to be extremely stiff from being in one position for so long." I nodded.

"Also, you need to continue taking it easy and not involve yourself in strenuous activities." He looked directly at Dree.

"What? She can't fuck her man or something?" His face was flushed with embarrassment. He ignored her and called a nurse in to assist with him taking the cast off.

125

"Ms. Anderson please be careful with any movement and I want you to set up an appointment to come back in two weeks. You'll need to set up physical therapy too."

"Girl, all the therapy you need is giving Frankie a hand job or.-"

"DREE!" I shouted.

"What? Shit, he knows what sex is, don't you doctor?"

"Ummm. Ms. Anderson take care and call me if you have any questions." He glanced over at Dree who stood up to take a call.

"Please don't bring her back." He whispered and I busted out laughing.

"I'll try not to but she drove me here."

"Ok but try and get back to driving." He was dead ass serious, which made it even funnier. He shook my good hand, took one last look at Dree who gave him a fake smile and stepped out.

"Bitch, you crazy." I told her and slowly got off the table.

"He'll be alright." She waved her hand in the air.

126

"You hungry?" I asked and grabbed the papers off the table.

"Hell yea bitch. I am pregnant." I rolled my eyes. Not because I'm jealous or anything like that but because she can never just say yes or no.

"Keep talking shit and I promise to tell SJ where we at." She gave me the finger but I bet her ass was quiet.

On the ride over to the restaurant, I spoke to Frankie and let him know the cast was off. He was happy because he knew how much it bothered me to have him helping. I needed him in the shower, to get dressed, cook and I even tried to clean and it was aggravating. I'm used to doing everything on my own. I won't ever take my body for granted when it comes to being able to use every limb. You never know how much you need each body part, until you can no longer use it.

She parked in a parking spot and came to help me out. I could do it but getting in and outta cars were hard too. I told her to wait until she gets bigger and can't do shit. She had to remind me, she's been there and done that but couldn't wait for me to experience it. I rolled my eyes and walked in front of her.

I had to run a little because a car came racing through the parking lot. I had no idea who it was and my anger went from zero to hundred when this dumb bitch stopped in front of me and rolled the window down.

"So, I see you're not incapacitated anymore."

"What the fuck you want?" Dree walked up on the driver's side and hit the bitch so hard, her head was almost in the passenger seat.

"She can't whoop your ass right now but I can."

"You stupid bitch. I can't believe you hit me." Crystal yelled and you saw her window go up and heard the doors locked. For her to be a punk, she talked mad shit. Dree tried hard as hell to open the door. Crystal's stupid ass had the nerve to stick her tongue out and put her hands up to her ear like a kid. *What the hell did Frankie see in this childish bitch?*

"Let's go Dree. You know she ain't doing shit."

"I'm gonna beat your ass the next time I see you." Crystal gave her the finger and cracked the passenger side window.

"I guess Frankie doesn't need my services anymore."

128

"Bitch, he been stopped using your dumb ass."

"Hmph. Not when he let me play with his dick in the parking lot of the Subway."

"What the fuck ever?"

"You don't have to believe me. You still have the same number, right?" I rolled my eyes and watched as she pulled her phone out.

"Let's go Lexi. You know he ain't cheating on you." Dree pushed me in the building but not after listening to Crystal scream out to check my phone. How did the bitch even get my number? I guess all the times Frankie and I spoke, she probably stole it from his phone.

I opened the message and the first one told me she paid someone to get the footage in case I'm wondering. The next one, showed a video of Frankie putting a bag in his truck and her in his face. I covered my mouth when it showed her hand go in his sweatpants. I knew the exact day this was because of the clothes he wore. Not only did he let her do that but he came to the hospital and I gave him head. He fell asleep next to me and never said a word about seeing her. Pissed, wasn't the word for the way I was feeling.

"Ugh, we're gonna take our order to go." Dree told the lady and ordered our usual. I sat on the bench and tried my best not to let a tear drop.

"Lexi, I know you're upset but he did push her off him. You can tell it was unexpected." Dree tried to make me see it in a different light.

"Dree, I get it and yes he did push her off but she shouldn't have even been close enough to do it. I know you can't stop spur of the moment things but he also knows she wants him so why even converse with her?"

"I can't even think about what I'd do and I get it. All I'm saying is, you're right. He shouldn't have been that close but aren't you the same person who told me I couldn't be mad at Whitney for making a copy of SJ's key and coming there naked. Shit, she had him hard as hell. Not that I'm looking but it doesn't seem like she made an impact on him."

"Why didn't he tell me?"

"I'm gonna play devil's advocate here." I sucked my teeth because she was always tryna be on both sides.

"One… he may not have told you because you were in the hospital and he didn't want you upset. And two… you gave that nigga some bomb ass head and put him to sleep." She made me laugh a little.

"Do you really think he was gonna bring it up after that?"

"He could've told me later."

"True and had nothing been going on, he probably would've." She stood to go get the food from the register.

"I know you're mad but go home and ask what happened. He may not have told you for the reasons I said. But I bet he apologizes and sucks the skin off your toes." I laughed so hard she had to pat my back. The chick at the register shook her head laughing too.

"Let's go. You got me cutting the fuck up today Lexi and the shit don't have anything to do with me."

"Whatever." She opened the door and we both stepped out.

"Are you going home or to my house?"

"I guess to yours since he isn't home yet."

"You do know I'm staying with my parents?" She reminded me because I did forget.

"Ughhhh. Is Dreek Jr. home?" I hated going over there when he was home. He'd bother me every time. One would assume its because he liked me but that's far from the case. He considered me his sister and said since we didn't grow up together he had to bother me for old times' sake. He would do annoying shit every time.

"Probably not. His girlfriend be sweating the shit outta him now that she's pregnant too."

"Thank goodness." We drove to her house, stepped out and went inside.

"Oh shit Lexi." Dreek Jr. surprised us at the door. It was just my luck he'd be here. Dree shrugged her shoulders and moved past me.

"Leave her alone Dreek. You stay bothering her." His girlfriend said and gave me a hug. They've been together for a few years and she was cool as hell.

132

"Please keep him away from me."

"I'll try." I gave her a look. We all knew how strung out they were on each other.

"I gave him some earlier. Shit, I be needing a break." I started laughing.

"I'm serious. That nigga will go all night if I let him." She shook her head when he came back over to where we were standing.

"Damn right I will." He wrapped his arms around her waist and kissed the back of her neck.

"I'm not gonna bother you today Lexi because you got that cast off but I will another time. I don't want you to get me arrested for messing with the disabled."

"WHAT?" He pointed to my arm.

"You see that shit ma?" He said to his girl.

"One arm is bigger than the other. You know the advocates for disabilities would try and throw the book at me if I bothered her. Plus, you know Frankie all extra sensitive when it comes to her." I gave him the finger and walked in the kitchen with Dree and her parents.

133

My arm was thinner than the other due to the cast but his ass didn't have to point it out. I grabbed my food and looked to see her dad all over her mom. I thought of my parents and smiled. After this shit with Rome, I pray Frankie and I have peace and have the same.

"Come on J. Dree here so lil man is fine. Just a few minutes." I was hysterical, where Dree sucked her teeth and left the room. She'll get over it just like I do. I sat my ass right there ate my food and disappeared to Dree's room to sleep. I'll deal with Frankie when I get up.

Frankie

"You gonna stop coming for my wife nigga." I said to Dreek Jr. who stayed messing with Alexis. Dree told me she was in her room taking a nap and her brother was bothering her as usual.

"Oh y'all got married?" He turned towards the kitchen.

"MA! Frankie and Lexi got married and didn't invite us." He yelled.

"WHAT?" His mom walked in the room with her arms folded.

"Now you know he's lying. Mrs. Puryear, I would've made sure you were first on the list."

"Ma, he said his wife."

"She is my wife nigga; ring or not. Ima about to..."

"You about to what?" His girl said waddling in the room. She stood in front of him and he was silently talking mad shit behind her. His mom popped him on the head.

"Nothing. I don't want no problems." I put my hand up in surrender.

"That's what I thought." She said and smirked.

"Y'all are perfect together." I said when she walked away.

"I got you later nigga."

"What the fuck ever. Nigga you still owe me a stack for me whooping yo ass in fort nite." I had one foot on the bottom step.

"Bro, you were fucking cheating." He put his hands up.

"Are you serious? Dude, you and I were playing against each other and you died first. How you still claiming different?"

"Whatever." I waved him off and heard him yell I better have his money next time. I ain't paying his punk ass shit

If you're wondering how we knew him, as you can tell he's Dreeka's brother and one of Kane's friends and he didn't have a lot. They met through Lexi and been down for each other ever since. But Dreek is just like his sister. They both got a smart-ass mouth and stay talking shit to people. However, they will rock someone quick as hell who fucks with their family and friends. No questions asked.

I walked up to Dree's room, opened the door and found my girl knocked out. You could see she was babying her arm because she was lying on her side and holding it with the other hand. I put her shoes on, lifted her up and carried her down the steps. She opened her eyes and kept her head on my shoulders. I'm surprised she didn't ask for a kiss like she usually did. We said goodbye to everyone and left.

The drive to Kane Jr's house was a quiet one. We had been staying between her parents and mine until we found this Rome nigga, who appeared to be gone with the wind. Anyway, once she told me the cast was off, I told her brother we were staying over there. He told me sleep on the other side of the house because he didn't wanna hear us and I felt the same. Raya is my cousin, just like Lexi is his sister and neither him or I wanted to hear them making any noises.

I put the car in park and went over to the other side to help her. She swatted my hand away and said she had it. I could tell something was up but I also know when she's ready to speak on it, she will. I closed the door and used her key to open Kane's. Him and Raya were on the couch watching television. They had a cover on them so it's no telling what they were doing underneath. I locked the door and we went to the bedroom we'd be staying in.

"When did you get this?" She finally spoke and pointed to the clothes on the bed.

"Earlier. Once you said the cast was off, I knew you'd want that pussy ate." She sucked her teeth. Any other time she's be all for it. That's how I know somethings wrong. I locked the bedroom door, shut the shower on and helped take her clothes off. Her attitude was felt the entire time but I had plans for her.

"Frankie what are you doing?" I had her backed into the wall with her legs wrapped around my waist. I could see her trying not to lift her arm.

"Tell me right now what's wrong or I promise to fuck the shit outta you." She remained quiet. Times like this, her nasty ass wanted it rough and that's exactly what I'm about to do.

138

"FUCKKKKKKK! GOT DAMMIT!" She screamed and bit down on my shoulder when I forcefully entered her.

"Tell me." She was still quiet and trying her hardest not to scream again.

I made sure she was secure in my arms, lifted her up and slammed her down harder. She came hard and smacked the hell outta me. Now, any other bitch would've made me knock her the fuck out. However, Lexi has never put hands on me and vice versa so something is really bothering her.

"Aight Lexi. Stop. You're gonna make me cum." She squeezed her muscles together and just like that, I came all inside her. I silently prayed she got pregnant again. I let her down and made her look at me.

"You let Crystal touch your dick." I could see her eyes watering.

"It was a mistake Lexi. I was picking the food up, she caught me off guard and wait! How did you know?" She punched me in the chest with her good hand.

"The dumb bitch showed me a video. Why didn't you stay away from her?"

"A video? Wasn't no one out there."

"Yea well. She paid someone to tape it." I felt my anger growing and grabbed the soap to wash us both up.

"Lexi, I was gonna tell you but when I got there, you were hungry and I wasn't tryna make you mad. Then you gave me some bomb ass head and put me to sleep. Did you really think I'd remember?"

"Fuck that Frankie you should've told me. Had me looking dumb as hell in front of her." I pulled her close.

"You can never look dumb Lexi. Listen to me." I used the knuckle on my index finger to lift her face.

"She caught me off guard and yes I should've told you. I apologize and it won't happen again. I love you too much and I'm not about to lose you."

"Frankie she..." I cut her off with a kiss.

"I don't care what she said or showed you. You're my woman and nothing her or any other woman does will make me cheat. We waited a long time to get where we are and nothing is going to hold us back." She nodded and stood on her tippy toes to kiss me.

"Wait right here." I stepped out with the soap still on, ran in the room, reached in my pocket and back in the bathroom I went.

"Lexi." She opened the glass door and covered her mouth.

"Alexis Anderson, we've been through a lot to be together but you are the only woman I want and need in my life. I wanna wake up and go to sleep with you right by my side every day and night. I wanna fill you up with babies and raise them with our two dogs and cat like you always wanted. And last but not least, I wanna make you my wife asap. Will you marry me?" The tears flowing down her face told me she was with it but the words wouldn't come out.

"I can't hear you."

"YES! BABY YES! YES! A HUNDRED TIMES YES!" She shouted and put her hand out for me to slide the ring on.

"I love you woman." I now had her in my arms and my face in the crook of her neck as she continued crying happy tears.

"Now can I eat that good ass pussy like I planned before you got mad?"

"I don't know. Can you?" She shut the shower water off and had me follow her in the room. Let's just say. The two of us had each other moaning most of the night and I wouldn't change a thing about it.

****

"How you feeling?" I asked Lexi the next day. After we finished going round for round, she complained of her arm hurting. The doctor told her it would be stiff but she managed to maneuver through sex fine.

"I'm ok. And you?" She had her arm out looking at the ring.

"Now that I know you're gonna be my wife, I'm perfect." She put her arm down and stared at me.

"Do you know Crystal is the one who told Rome where we stayed?"

"Yea right. That bitch didn't know where we lived."

"That's what I thought until she followed you."

142

"Say what?" She told me about the conversation the two of them had in the truck. Crystal was a piece of work and I'm gonna make sure she regrets ever putting Lexi in danger. I hated to hear the nigga wanted to sleep with her after Crystal gave him head though. What type of nigga does that? But then again, my girl had some banging ass pussy. I'm mad as hell he had it and even angrier he reminisced over it. I had a trick for both of their asses tho.

We put some clothes on and walked downstairs only to find Raya and Kane coming out his room. She had on some leggings and a t shirt and all he had on were some sweats. Unfortunately, with her leg being broken he had to carry her down the steps but he didn't seem to mind. I guess they are in love. You have to be, to deal with a woman not being able to move and have to be carried everywhere.

"OH MY GODDDDDD! YOU'RE ENGAGED!" Raya shouted when she saw Lexi's hand.

"It's about time nigga. Tha fuck took you so long?" Kane said looking at the ring.

"I had to find the perfect one."

143

"How much was it?" Raya asked, as if I'd tell her.

"Raya really?" Kane put a chair under her leg at the table. The wheelchair was in the living room but he told me she had been refusing to sit in it unless necessary.

"I'll say no amount of money is too much to spend on Lexi."

"Bro, you already got the pussy and she said yes. You don't need to sugar coat shit." He opened the fridge and took some food out. I didn't say anything because it was true. I can't wait for his ass to propose to someone. I'm gonna be all in his shit the same way.

"Lexi you cooking right?" She sucked her teeth and took the stuff out his hand.

"I'll help you Lexi. We're gonna be related soon anyway."

"Kane, you asked her to marry you?" Lexi was overly excited.

"What the hell you talking about? Her and Frankie cousins. Duh!" I saw the way my cousin looked at him and so did he.

"Don't worry Raya. When it's my turn to propose, I'm gonna do it big."

"Oh you're marrying me?" She questioned and started cracking the eggs Lexi placed in front of her in the bowl. Kane kneeled down in front of her.

"Hell yea I'm marrying you. Ain't no other nigga ever getting in between these thighs. That pussy belongs to me. I been tatted my name on it." And just like that Raya was happy again.

"I don't wanna hear that shit." I went over to grab some potatoes to cut up.

"And we didn't wanna hear y'all motherfuckers moaning all night either." I busted out laughing.

"Don't laugh. I had to turn the television up."

"Kane don't be like that. We were doing the same thing. They couldn't hear us because you turned the TV up."

"You talk too much Raya." He stood over by the counter and answered his phone. The three of us were talking and stopped when we noticed Kane's face.

"What's wrong?" Lexi asked.

145

"That was pop pop. Your grandmother had a heart attack."

"Why she gotta be my grandmother?"

"She damn sure ain't mine and you knew her first." He shrugged his shoulders and moved to where Raya was.

"Are you going to see her?" Raya asked and the two of them stared at each other. Once Kane smirked, I knew it was over for their grandmother. May God rest her soul.

Lexi

I admit hearing my grandmother had a heart attack bothered me some. But then I remembered how much pain she's caused this family. Did I want her to die? No but whether the Lord takes her or my father, she'll be outta here soon.

The only reason my dad hasn't done it yet is because he's scared to leave my mom's side. The bullet exploded in her stomach and did more damage than we knew. It was gonna take her months to recover and my father is taking it extremely hard.

He continues to blame himself for allowing my mom to keep the kids around her all these years. It's crazy because no matter how mean she was to my mother; my mom never responded with hatred unless she attacked one of us or spoke about me not biologically being hers. To this very day, we have no idea why my grandmother is the way she is but the one thing my mom won't allow, is for us to bad talk her. One would think after everything she's said and done, she'd be the first but nope. My mom said God will handle it and now look. She's laid up in the hospital and none of us are eager to see her.

After eating breakfast, I asked Frankie to drop me by my parents' house. My mother came home from the hospital a few days ago and my dad refused to allow Kane and I over. He said the other kids wanted to be around her too and that he wasn't sharing his bed with us again. He speaks of us being spoiled when he's just as bad.

"You want me to come in?"

"If you want but I'm gonna probably be in the room with her."

"Aight. Hit me when you're ready and Lexi." He put his hand on my arm before I got out.

"Yes."

"I love you baby and I'm gonna find that bitch Crystal and the fuck nigga. I'm gonna make sure they die and can't bother us any longer." I pecked his lips.

"Hurry up because I wanna go back home. That's my house Frankie and I don't want to live away from it." I was getting upset. That was the house we had built together. Every detail, the paint, decorations, and furniture all came from our ideas and I'll be damned if we can't live in it due to this bitch being jealous and Rome being mad his father died.

"I promise we'll be back home soon."

"I believe you. Just hurry up. I wanna lay-up with my fiancé so he can get me pregnant. I wanna walk around naked and give you head in the hallway just because."

"Stop talking baby. My dick getting hard." I smiled.

"I got you later."

"You better after talking like that." We kissed again and I stepped out. He waited for me to go in before pulling off. My younger siblings ran over to hug me and I caught my dad in the kitchen. He was on his way to the basement and I'm positive it's too smoke.

"Daddy." He turned around when his foot hit the last step.

"I'm about to smoke. Is it important?"

"I just wanted to tell you I'm going to see grandma later. Can you take me?" I asked with a grin on my face.

"We'll go after I smoke this." I nodded, closed the door and went upstairs to check on my mom. She was sitting in the recliner my dad got for her with her legs up. The television was on and she had the iPad in her lap and the phone next to her. Her hair was in a ponytail and she had on a sweat suit. Even though she was shot, my mom was still the bomb.

"Hey honey. Let me pass this board and we can talk." I had to laugh because my mom gets addicted to those games. After she finished and looked up at me, she already knew before I could open my mouth.

"Make sure each of you are safe and no one gets caught. I am not capable of coming to get any of you outta jail."

"Ma, I didn't say a word."

"I'm your mother Lexi. You don't have to." I pulled the ottoman from in front of their bed and placed it next to her. I let my head fall on her shoulder and felt one of her hands running through my hair.

"I can't save her from your father or brother anymore." I looked up at her.

"I've dealt with a lotta things from her but sending that man's son after you and my husband is where I draw the line." I noticed the tears coming down.

"Ma."

"I'm serious Lexi. The constant reminders of you not biologically being mine hurt more than you could imagine." She held my face in her hands.

"I may not have birthed you but you've been my child since you were two. My name is on all your paperwork and I would never change anything."

"I know ma."

"I love you, your brothers and sisters so much. It bothers me that she couldn't be civil even if it were just for the kids."

"Why are you crying? Are you in pain?" My father rushed over when he came in the room.

"No babe. I was just telling Lexi that whatever you choose to do I'm fine with. Just don't go to jail. I can't get you out while I'm like this."

"April, it's gonna be ok and I'll be home soon."

"Kane." He kneeled in front of her.

"Would you still do anything for me?" He had a grin on his face.

"I'd do anything plus some." She pulled him on for a kiss but just a peck. Thank goodness because I didn't wanna see all that extra stuff they do.

"I know she's your mom but if you don't do it; I will." We both looked at her.

"April."

"I mean it. I'm done dealing with her and.-"

"Don't say anymore. Your husband will always have your back." He shushed her with his finger.

"I'm not blaming you for how she treated you or anything else for that matter. You went above and beyond and it was for nothing. I'm gonna do what should've been done a long time ago." He glanced over at me.

"You ready?" I nodded and stood.

"Watch over my babies Kane."

"Babies? Only Lexi's coming." She turned her lips up.

"Trust that my son's coming too if he doesn't beat you there."

"Shit!" He said and ran down the steps. I kissed my mom on the cheek and told her I'd watch over them. Hell, I ain't killing no one. I hopped in the car and laid my head on the seat; waiting to see how it'll all play out.

****

"Why are we stopping here?" I asked my dad when we pulled up to some house.

"I need to pick something up."

"What?" I stared into the fucked up yard and at the abandoned looking house. I've never even been to this area so why he was, is beyond me.

"Don't ask questions."

"Daddy."

"Look my nosy child." I sucked my teeth.

"I may not be in the game but I still know a lotta people and have some who will ride for me." I gave him a crazy look.

"You better not tell April either." He went to get out and I placed my hand on his arm.

153

"What?"

"Does mommy know I consider her my mom?" He looked at me.

"Of course, she does."

"No, I mean does she know I consider her my birth mother?"

"Huh?" I could see the confusion on his face.

"I don't even associate Erica with being the woman who had me in her stomach." I hated Erica and the reason I referenced her by her first name is because she didn't deserve for me to call her mother.

"Lexi, I know what Erica did was wrong and she paid for it with her life but she is biologically your mother."

"No she's not." I pouted and folded my arms.

"If you don't wanna ever claim her, then don't but I also need you to know that April never tried to take her place. She raised you as her own and called you her daughter but she never wanted you to assume she was tryna take over."

"I didn't think that."

"I know and she does now too." He turned my face to look at him.

"Lexi, April always wanted to make sure you felt no different because you didn't come from her womb, which is why she made sure to go to war over anyone for mentioning it or bothering you."

"I understand but I wanna keep it the way it was, of no one knowing she didn't physically have me."

"No one knows and as far as I'm concerned, they never will. Where is all this coming from? You've been comfortable with her position as your mom since you were young."

"I think its because grandma hurt her so much, I didn't want her thinking I felt the same way."

"I can tell you that without a shadow of a doubt she is your mother and doesn't think that way. Shit, 99% of the time I can't tell she isn't."

"So the one percent is what?"

"The one percent is because I had to put my foot down a few times and tell her to stop spoiling you. I felt she was trying too hard to make you feel loved."

"Really?"

"Yes. Especially when the other kids came. She made sure to go outta her way for you, even when you didn't deserve it."

"Huh?"

"You would get in trouble as a kid and she'd take up for you everytime. Then you had a fit when Kane Jr. was born and required all of her time. She'd make me keep Kane away in the other room sometimes just to make sure you were happy."

"I didn't know that or should I say, I don't remember."

"You were young Lexi. All you saw was April loving you and giving you what you wanted. She doesn't regret it and she'd do it all again for you." I don't know why but I just started crying. I really loved her and him mentioning this only made me love her even more if that's even possible.

"Do me a favor and don't bring it up to her. She doesn't like to be told because she felt, she neglected Kane Jr. and your other siblings at times and it bothers her."

"If you ask me, I don't think she neglected Kane Jr. enough." He laughed.

"I know. That nigga will not get off my wife's titty." I busted out laughing and he told me to wait in the car.

I watched him go to the door and slap hands with another older guy. About five minutes later he came out with a small black pouch in his hand and the same guy smoking. My dad stayed getting high. He says it's the only way to keep him calm and where we're going, he's gonna definitely need to be relaxed.

He finished with the guy, slapped hands and sat down in the car.

"What's this?" He snatched it out my hand.

"Stop touching shit."

"Sorry. What is it though?"

"Your grandmothers fate." Is all he said and pulled off. I can't wait to see what it is.

Kane Jr.

"I'll see you in a few." I sat Raya down in the living room of her parents' house. Once Lexi left, I knew it was a matter of time before she and my father made it to the hospital. I refused to allow that woman to breathe another day. If my father planned on taking her life, I wanted to witness it myself.

All the hurt and pain she caused my mom and sometimes my sister, deserves for her to disappear. I say my sister because she felt some kinda way about how my grandmother always mentioned my mom not being hers. She'd cry and run to our mom and ask why my father didn't meet her first. It was always sad and my mom would cry with her. Its about time karma stepped in and let her feel the pain and her karma, is me or my pops if he beat me there.

"Are you gonna be ok?" I never hid anything from her so she knew exactly where I was going.

"I'm good."

"You sure?" I let a smile creep on my face. I was in love with her and everyday it felt as if I were falling deeper. I know she feels the same because she expressed it last night after we had each other moaning. We could only give each other oral sex because of her broken leg. She tried to get me to make love to her but I couldn't. The way I like to flip her ass would damn sure make it hurt worse.

"It has to be done and yes I'm ok. I promise to call you soon as it's finished." She nodded and I leaned down for a kiss. I heard someone clear their throat and it was her father. He knows what it is but we tried to keep it PG in front of him.

"Let your father know Arnold and I have people watching so no one comes in. Call me when it's done so I can send somebody over to make sure it's considered an accident." I thought about questioning him but Arnold is his brother and I'm sure he spoke to my father. Like I stated before, our fathers aren't best friends but they are cool and we look out for each other.

"Thanks, and I'll tell him as soon as I get there. Can you make sure my girl doesn't try walking?" He gave Raya a hard stare and she rolled her eyes at me.

Over the last few days, she's been trying hard to walk. However, she still has the arm cast on and the doctor said she couldn't use crutches because it would bare too much weight it won't heal correctly. I didn't want her to waste any more time in a cast if she didn't have to.

"I got her. Keep an eye on your surroundings and I'll see you later." I gave him my thanks and walked out. I felt my phone vibrating as I sat in my truck and look down.

Raya: *I miss you already*. A smile graced my face.

Me: *Same here*.

Raya: *Hurry up back so I can release the stress that's gonna build up*." My dick twitched after reading it.

Me: *You don't have to tell me twice.* I put the phone in my pocket and drove to the hospital.

When I got there, I parked on a side street to keep my truck from being seen. I stepped out, pulled my cap down and made my way inside. I asked the receptionist which floor she was on and gave her a fake name. The less information linked to me, the better. I took the stairs and once I stepped on the floor, my father and sister were standing there grinning.

160

"What?"

"We knew your ass would be here." I laughed and asked why they were outside in the lobby.

"We waited because I didn't need your ass busting in while I'm doing it." My father said.

"We have to wait for SJ anyway." I shrugged my shoulders and sat in one of the chairs.

"Its ok. Pop pop in there right now." Lexi said and I looked up at her.

"Really?" I questioned and my dad had me move to the corner with him. My grandfather is the one who contacted me but I didn't know he was here. I mean she is still his wife because she was adamant about not signing the divorce papers. She told my grandfather the only way he'd leave her is in death. I guess he'll be free of her soon enough.

"He knows what's about to go down." My eyes grew big.

"And what he say?"

"Nothing he can say. He knew, like my mother knows, that this day would come. Unfortunately, it should've been sooner but with your mom getting shot, I had to wait. And you know there's no time like the present." He patted my shoulder and answered his phone. My mom was calling and its most likely to make sure none of us were in jail.

"I didn't miss it, did I?" SJ came strolling in slowly with Dree next to him. He was still moving at a sluggish pace due to the shooting.

"Nah, we were waiting on you." Dree had a confused look on her face. He must not have told her and asked her to stay outside until we came out.

"Y'all ready?" My father asked and we all shook our head. I know it sounds fucked up to kill her but as you read in book one and in the Let Me Be The One series, my grandmother's a bitch and more than deserves this.

Lexi told Dree she'd be back and to text her if she saw anything out the ordinary, which reminded me about Raya's dad. I'll tell my pops afterwards.

We made our way down the hall and stopped in front of her door. My grandfather was sitting in a chair watching television. He noticed us, stood, kissed my grandmother on the forehead and walked out. He told us he'd be in the waiting room. Its crazy how he was ok with it but then again, he had no choice either.

The moment we stepped in, my grandmother began to panic. You could hear the machines going haywire but not one nurse or doctor came in, which is weird.

"Hello mother. It doesn't look like you're happy to see us." My dad ran his hand down her face.

"What… what… are you doing here?" She sat up and tried to press the nurses button but I snatched it out her hand. SJ leaned over and pulled the plug from the wall to stop the beeping of the machines.

"This is what's gonna happen mother." My father moved over to the spot where her IV was. SJ and I stood there waiting to see what he had planned. We knew he was gonna take her life but never said how.

"You're gonna tell me why you hated my wife so much. Then I wanna know why you sent that niggas son after me and my daughter? At last but not least, I wanna know why you didn't love me." He opened the black pouch and pulled a syringe out.

"Kane please." She tried to grab his hand and he snatched away.

"To be honest ma, you should've been dead."

"Excuse me."

"I planned on killing you a long time ago but my wife. You know the one you hate so much; stopped me." She rolled her eyes.

"She said, Kane let your mother be. It's who she is and I don't have to be around her." He sat on the bed and stared at her.

"Now. Let me hear it."

"Hear what?" Did she really pretend not to know what he spoke of?

"Why didn't you like my wife and send that nigga's son after me and my daughter? Oh, and why didn't you love me?"

"I did love you Kane. How can you say that?"

"You got two minutes to explain yourself." He glanced down at his watch.

"I loved April at one point but then you came home and she took all your time and attention. You barely called or stopped by and it bothered me." All of us looked at her like she was crazy.

"When the stuff happened with Lexi, I thought you would blame her and come around me more. When you didn't, I blamed her. Then, I tried to break the bond between Lexi and April and it lasted all of a week or two because she cried for her."

"So you did all this over jealousy?" I saw my dad's fist ball up. I looked behind me and Lexi had her own tears falling down her face.

"I don't expect you to understand but I missed you all those years you were in prison."

"But you came to see me."

"It wasn't enough. I wanted more time and you were always with her." She wiped her eyes.

"How did you find that nigga?"

"After the Glen guy disappeared I never thought about him again; until Lexi was in college." I heard my sister yell out what and SJ stood in front of her. Regardless of her arm still being stiff she was ready to fight.

"I saw him in the mall and he resembled Glen. Before you ask, I'll never forget his face."

"What did you say to him?" My pops leg was shaking.

"I offered him a deal." She stopped and observed everyone in the room. I think she was looking for a way out if you ask me.

"Don't stall. What deal did you offer?" She immediately started crying.

"What deal?"

"He was to meet Lexi and get to know her. Once he met the family, he was supposed to kill April."

"WHAT?" My father's hands were around her throat.

"Pops, stop. You can't have prints on her neck or it won't look accidental."

"DO YOU KNOW HE SHOT MY WIFE? SHE ALMOST DIED BECAUSE OF YOU." SJ and I pried his hands off. I heard a noise like someone hitting the wall. Lexi was hysterical sliding down to the floor. Her knees were against her chest and her chin was in top of them.

"I'm sorry Kane. She was always there and.-" My dad was passed angry. None of us ever witnessed this side of him. He had days where he may have been mad, but this was different. He had to be in a zone.

"I love you Kane. I'm so sorry." He snatched away from us and picked the syringe up.

"You don't love anyone but yourself. Enjoy hell." He injected the serum slow. We all turned our heads when the door opened.

SJ

"Is she dead yet?" My father asked as my mom wheeled him in. He was still in the hospital recovering because he was hit way more than I was. When he woke from the coma a week ago, the doctor wanted him to stay a little longer.

"She's on her way." Kane Jr. said and my uncle continued ignoring him and staring at my grandmother. Whatever he gave her, was taking its time to work.

"Don't you think we should've discussed this?" He said and my uncle fucking snapped. He jumped in my father's face and all of us were nervous. I couldn't do shit because I wasn't fully healed yet. Kane Jr. didn't know if he should stand in the way or not. Lexi and my mom moved away and my grandmother sat there with tears coming down her face.

"Discuss what nigga? How she admitted to sending that boy's son to kill my wife? How she was jealous because she claimed April kept me away from her? Or how, for years she tormented, taunted, harassed, belittled, degraded and humiliated my wife? How about her tryna make my own kids hate their mother? What the fuck is there to discuss?"

"We're brothers nigga and she's my mother too."

"Brothers eh?" My uncle chuckled.

"I don't have one. I'm out."

"Kane." My dad grabbed his hand and had my mom not stepped in, I'm not sure what my uncle would've done.

"Once you disrespected my wife and tried to come for my son, you relinquished all your brotherly rights."

"Pops." Kane Jr. tried to speak.

"Nah son. He did this shit before and I told him back then, never to come for my wife and family again."

"Kane, she's our mother and you have to see it from my point."

"I don't have to see shit because if she came for Essence the way she came for April, I'd have her back too. But not you nigga. You took shit out on my wife that had nothing to do with her."

"No I didn't."

169

"My, how we forget but I'm gonna refresh your memory real quick." He looked at my cousin who was now hugging my mom.

"Lexi had just been attacked for the second time, April was pregnant with my son and I still came to be my brother's keeper. And what happened?" My uncle leaned down to my pops level.

"You accused me of being happy Essence left you, as if I gave a fuck. Then told me I was leaving to be with my girl, knowing we had family shit."

"Kane." My father tried to speak and my uncle shut him down again.

"Her fucking mother was shot and you didn't care. Stacy, you were a selfish motherfucker then and you're a selfish motherfucker now." He headed to the door and turned around.

"And you damn right I didn't ask you. I mean what for? You'd try to talk me out of it and it's no way in hell I'd let that bitch stay alive."

"Are you serious Kane?" My father just couldn't shut up. My uncle ran up on him.

"NIGGA MY WIFE ALMOST DIED! MY DAUGHTER WAS SLEEPING WITH A NIGGA WHOSE FATHER VIOLATED HER? WHY IN THE HELL WOULD YOU QUESTION ANYTHING?" No one said a word. My uncle's chest was rising and falling fast. He was ready to whoop my dad's ass and we all knew it.

"Daddy, I'm ready." Lexi said and took his hand in hers. He looked down at her and smiled. You could see him calming down. My uncle cherished his family and I couldn't understand why my pops didn't. I'm not saying he doesn't love us but it makes me wonder if he'd even confront his mother if she did the same things to my mom, that she did to April.

"It's about time." Kane Jr. said and we all looked at my grandmother who was now foaming at the mouth. She appeared to be having a seizure but the way her body jerked it looked crazy. We all stood there watching until she took her last breath. Lexi and my uncle left without saying a word.

"I'll see you later." Kane Jr. said. He gave my mom a hug, me a pound and my father a disgusted look. He picked his phone up and started texting away.

"He should've told me." My father said still tryna make what my uncle did wrong and not my grandmother.

"Stacy shut the fuck up."

"What?" He looked at my mom.

"You heard me. You always have something to say. Kane didn't tell you because even after everything that went down. After finding out the lengths she went through to destroy his relationship; you're still tryna defend her."

"That's not it. I wanted to say goodbye."

"For what though?" I asked because I needed to know.

"Are y'all forgetting she is still my mother?"

"And?" We both said at the same time.

"And he should've given me the time."

"Uncle Kane is never gonna speak to you again and I don't blame him."

"Fuck him. At this point, I don't even care anymore." My poos was talking big shit now that my uncle was gone.

172

"And that's what sad." I told him and started walking to the door.

"You can stay in denial but I tell you what?" I stopped next to him.

"You got one time for my mother to call and say you breathed on her wrong. I promise to kill you and shed tears as I sit in the front row of your funeral." He looked at me and my mom smirked. She knew I'd do anything for her; including kill. My pops can talk all the shit he wants but he knows I'm not playing.

"You ok?" Dree rushed over to me when I stepped out the room.

"I'm fine. I need to lay down for a bit." She held my hand and the two of us walked out like the happy couple we are; well should be.

We hadn't spoken since the shit with Melody in the parking lot. I had to practically beg her to pick me up. Frankie was dealing with some other shit and couldn't take me. She was the only one I could call. I had to send a text like it was an emergency just to get her to call me.

The shit with Melody was not what it seemed. Yes, I ran into her but all that rekindling the romance crap she spoke of, was a lie. She tried to get me to fuck her but I wasn't biting. I knew all about her and Herb. They got married a year or two ago. I never mentioned it to Dree because they weren't together so what's the purpose. I understood why she was upset; especially after hearing their kids were the same age. I still don't get why she ain't let me explain.

"Everything ok?" She asked when she jumped on the driver's side.

"It will be. Why you ask?" She started the car and backed outta the parking spot.

"I saw your uncle and Lexi leave. He didn't look happy and clearly, she was upset. Kane Jr. nodded and went past me and he always got something smart to say. And you look like it's a lot on your mind."

"Very observant I see." I heard her suck her teeth.

"Family shit. I'll tell you after you ride my dick." She snapped her head.

"I don't care how mad you are. I need to bust a nut and you're the only one who can do it."

"SJ."

"Fuck that. Pull this shit over." She ignored me so I grabbed the steering wheel.

"STOP IT!" She frantically yelled and I kept doing it.

"Ok I'll stop. Hold on." She parked on a side street.

"You wanna ride me or am I coming on that side and fuck you?"

"SJ were not having sex." I reached over, snatched the keys out and walked to her side. I opened the door she tried to hold and slid her legs to the side. I gave zero fucks about her wearing jeans and gently pulled her out the truck.

"SJ." She tried to move my hands and I popped her. Once I got one pant leg down, I slid her panties to the side, pulled my dick out and rammed myself in her.

"Shit, I missed this." She moaned out.

"I know but I'm about to cum so don't get used to it." I fucked her harder and she was lucky she came before me because I damn sure bust fast.

"You should be ashamed of yourselves." I heard and turned around to see some white lady on the side of us.

"Why is that?" I turned around still zipping my jeans.

"You're having sex outside for God's sake." She said with her face turned up.

"We like to do things spontaneously and plus her pussy good as fuck. If I wanna stick my dick in her at a fucking playground, I will." Dree smacked my arm.

"Nah, fuck her old ass."

"Excuse me!" She grabbed her chest and pulled off.

"The bitch was probably watching. Now get yo ass in the car so we can discuss this Melody shit. I'm tired of sleeping alone and having a hard dick in the morning." She sucked her teeth and jumped in the driver's seat. I closed the door and got in. She can pretend not to want me but her ass ain't going nowhere.

Dree

I can't stand when SJ acts like he running shit. Granted, I placed myself in the truck but I needed a ride home. If he let me drive I'd surely pull up at my parents' house and not this damn hotel.

"Let's go." He put the keys in his pocket and stepped out. I thought about staying inside but did I really feel like arguing or wrestling with him today?

He took my hand in his and the two of us walked straight to the elevators. I'm guessing this is where he's been staying when he's not over his parents. It was very nice and you could tell by the lobby and even the elevators this spot is expensive. The glass mirrors against the wall made me look fat as hell. My stomach had a small pouch but if I went off this mirror, I'd swear I was at least five or six months. SJ must've noticed me staring and placed his hand on my belly from behind.

"You're not fat Dree."

"I didn't say anything."

"You don't have to. I see your face." He turned me around as the doors opened.

"You look beautiful and when my baby gets bigger in your stomach, you'll still be beautiful to me."

"Awwww baby." I was about to wrap my arms around his neck but he let me go to catch the doors from closing.

"Come on." We stepped off and again I remained in awe of this hotel. Everything about it was perfect, even down to the rugs.

I heard the beeping noise from the door and stepped in behind him. There was a living room, kitchen, small dining area and bathroom. He walked me up the short staircase and the bed was humongous. I noticed the balcony door and went over to see what's below. There was a pool, hot tub and basketball court off the side. Thank goodness I've never been here because I probably wouldn't leave.

"I got good and expensive taste." He winked and removed all his clothes. I knew he was weak from the shooting but I had no idea he still had bandages on.

"I'm good Dree." He said when I asked if he needed to change them.

"You sure?"

"Yea. Take a shower with me." Before I could protest, my clothes were hitting the floor.

"SJ." I moaned out the second he dropped to his knees and placed my leg on his shoulder. He started sucking on my treasure and pulled a strong orgasm out. I say strong because I literally felt my body jerk, shake and I slid down the wall. Had he not caught me, I would've bust my ass.

"Damn baby, you needed that." I smacked his chest as he helped me up.

"I missed this." He had me turned around with both hands squeezing my ass. He spread my cheeks opened and wasted no time plunging into his favorite place. I had to use my hand to hold him back a little because of how hard he went. I missed him too but got damn.

SMACK! SMACK! SMACK! Each time he did it, my clit grew harder.

"That's right Andreeka. Cum for your man." His arm was around my stomach while his fingers worked wonders on my nub.

"Come on ma. Stop playing." He circled faster and penetrated me harder. I could feel him twitching inside and placed my hand under my body to play with his balls.

"Fuck Dree. Shit! I'm about to cum."

"Me too SJJJJJJJJJJ!" I couldn't hold out any longer and ejected all my cream onto him. I felt his warm juices filling my insides up.

"Let me wash you up. I wanna fuck the shit outta you on the balcony." He said.

"SJ, I don't think..." I made the attempt to tell him I needed a break but he cut me off with his lips crashing on mine. Needless to say, I got no break and by the time he was finished with me, a bitch went straight to sleep.

****

"Dree, I didn't sleep with Melody." SJ looked up from his breakfast to tell me. Once I fell asleep, we both knew neither of us would be up until the next day.

"Why did you say no one occupied your time when we broke up?" I was a little emotional.

"Because no one did. What Melody told you is partly true." I dropped my fork, leaned back in the chair and waited to hear his reason.

"Melody and I did run into one another when you broke up with me. She asked if we could meet up for drinks and I agreed." I rolled my eyes.

"Anyway, she told me about how her man cheated on her a few times, had more kids and was staying out later and later. Now me, I don't give a fuck and couldn't understand why she was telling me." He put some bacon in his mouth.

"Then she proceeds to say they were married for almost two years now but that she wanted to get revenge, which is where I came in."

"Say what?" I sat up in the chair.

"Exactly! She wanted me to sleep with her so she could use it against him."

"Did you?"

"Honestly Dree. I thought about it." I sucked my teeth.

"I mean, why not? You left me, we were drinking and I was horny so I should just do it." He moved closer to me.

"But I couldn't do it because regardless if we were together or not, you were still my woman and I refused to cheat." I could feel the grin creeping on my face.

"Plus, after having you and doing all the freaky things we do, I knew for a fact the sex wouldn't be worth it." I stood and sat on his lap.

"But she said you cheated on her. It's what you do."

"I did cheat on her but it's because we were young and the shit with Whitney is because she let me." He shrugged his shoulders.

"I know for a fact you won't allow me to do you that way and stick around."

"Ugh no."

"And I'm not tryna lose you so ain't no way I'm risking this." He put his hand under the T-shirt he gave me to wear last night and slid his index finger in between my folds.

"I'm not risking this pussy for no bitch."

"You better not." My bottom half had a mind of its own as it began grinding on the two fingers he placed inside.

"You better not risk this dick either."

"Never baby. Mmmmmmm. It feels good." I let my lips find his and allowed him to bring me to a release.

"I do love you Dree."

"I love you too SJ."

"Then don't believe everything you hear and give me a chance to explain before going off the deep end."

"I will and I'm sorry. It's just this dick is so fucking good. I don't want anyone else to get it." I used my hand to place him inside.

"Ain't no one else getting it and shitttttt." He grabbed my hips and thrusted harder under me.

"I'm putting another baby in you after this one drops."

"SJ, that's too fast."

183

"Well you better get on birth control the second he pulls my son or daughter out because once I get the green light to go back in, a nigga is not pulling out." He stood me up against the wall and had me screaming, moaning and scratching his back. I loved the hell outta this man and prayed he felt the same like he says.

Rome

"Yo if you use your teeth on my dick again, I swear I'm gonna knock your head off." I told the Crystal bitch when I yanked her up by the hair.

"I was trying something new."

"Bitch if I want you to try something new, I'll tell you. Until then; continue sucking me off the way you been doing." I released her hair and laid my head back on the couch. Besides giving me good head and pussy on demand, I had nothing in common with this chick.

"Yea like that." I stared down at her and she was doing her thing. I felt my nut coming up and placed my hand on back of her head. For some reason she had a tendency of stopping. It's already hard to make a nigga cum like this but when a bitch can do it, the least she can do is swallow.

"Damnnn, that was good." I pushed her off and pulled my boxers and jeans up to answer the door someone was pounding on. Unfortunately, I been holed up in this hotel about two hours away from Lexi's just to stay outta sight until I get her father.

The night at the hospital when the shooting took place, I was shot in the leg. I can't even tell you who did it because it was so much going on and everyone had guns. The doctor gave me ten stitches and told me the bullet just missed a major artery. Any closer and I would've bled out. Thankfully, it didn't but I still have a slight limp due to it. I am shocked none of it made the news but knowing them, I'm not surprised.

I made my way to the door and looked out the peephole. This corny nigga and some chick stood there looking nervous as fuck. I never understood why people made shit obvious.

I opened the door and they both walked in. He glanced over to Crystal and shook his head. The chick sucked her teeth, which told me they were affiliated in some way. The woman was pretty and had a bad ass body but she wasn't my type. Any chick who hung with a corny ass dude like this guy, is probably a gold digger. I may have some money but ain't no bitch taking shit I worked for.

"What up?" I closed the door.

"Rome, this is Whitney. Whitney, this is Rome." I nodded and she slammed her body into the chair.

"What the fuck wrong with her?"

"She in her feelings because the nigga she loves, don't want her."

"Fuck you Herb. SJ with the bitch you love so don't talk shit." She rolled her eyes.

"SJ?" I questioned to make sure I heard her correctly.

"Yea." She had the nerve to get mad.

"This bitch set his house on fire and even set him up for me to kill him, but claiming she loves him. If that's love, I don't want it." Herb said and we both laughed.

"Hell no." I sat on the couch.

"I love you Rome. You wouldn't want me to help you set anyone up?" I looked at Crystal and realized she is as dumb as Lexi said she is.

"How you love me and you already set Frankie up when you led me to his house." I saw the Whitney chick's mouth drop.

"Love doesn't have a time limit and I'll do anything to kill that bitch."

"You love me Crystal?" I stared at her.

"Of course, I do." She let her hand roam my chest.

"You don't love no one but that Frankie nigga."

"Really Rome? We have a connection but you keep fighting it." I busted out laughing.

"Bitch bye."

"Bitch?" She stood like she had an attitude.

"You heard me. Don't try and impress these motherfuckers with some fantasy about us being together because we ain't like that." She stormed in the bathroom and slammed the door.

"Well ok then. What's on the agenda for Frankie and SJ?" Herb asked and Whitney looked up.

"Right now, my main concern is the father. I need his ass ASAP."

"Ok but can't we get him with those two?" Whitney questioned as if she had a say so. I don't even know why he brought her here anyway.

"Yea but the question is how? Lexi is with them so who else can we use to lure one, if not both of them in?"

"We can probably get Crystal to bring Frankie but her dumb ass blew it with SJ." Herb pointed to Whitney who flipped him the finger.

He called and told me how she asked him to help her get SJ, which is all good but he's the stupid one. I get you wanna do the whole revenge thing on the boss who stole your woman but Whitney went to his ex's house. He should've never let that happen because he has a kid with her. What if she tossed the cocktail in the house and his kid died? He was so busy acting on impulse, he just let her do whatever.

I give him credit for ambushing that nigga and his pops tho. Not that they did a good job because he never should've been able to pull out the driveway but then again, I missed the nigga who killed my father. It don't really matter because the way he dropped when her body hit the floor gave me an extensive amount of joy. I can't say I killed her but the damage definitely had to be bad.

Now I have these three idiots in front of me waiting on a clue. One would think that being though Herb worked for SJ, he'd know where his stash was or even the drop off and pickup dates. This nigga was making money and yet, had no information nothing. When he was an employee all he did was get a call to pick the product up, drop the money off and bounce.

"Yo, where did you say the warehouse is at?" I asked to see if he knew that much.

"It's pretty far. Why, you thinking about hitting it up?" He had a grin on his face.

"Do you think they'll have anything in there? Matter of fact, let's go see what they got and burn it down. We can wait in the cut for then to come and blast em." A grin creeped on my face thinking about getting those niggas. It may not be Lexi's father but his time for sure is coming.

****

"Yea ma." I answered because she called back over and over.

"Get to my place NOW!" She screamed before hanging up. I tried calling back but she didn't answer. I grabbed what I needed from the hotel and left.

It took me an hour to get over to my mom's because I was so far away. When I did, there were cops, a few detectives pulling away and I saw my kids. Usually the dumb baby mom I have, calls to tell me when she's dropping them off.

I reached out for my son and kissed my daughter on the cheek. The look of aggravation plagued my mom's face, which meant something bad happened and she's most likely gonna blame me.

"Someone killed her." My mom whispered.

"Killed who and why my kids here?" She shook her head and stepped inside with me behind her.

I placed my son the ground to crawl and my daughter was still in my mom's arms. At first, she didn't say much. When she gets like this, it means she's tryna get her words together or calm down. Not sure where her head is at but I wish she spit it out.

"What did you do?" She finally spoke.

"As far as?" I walked in the kitchen to grab something to drink.

"Somebody killed their mother." She pointed to my kids. She couldn't stand my baby moms and hated to even sat her name.

"WHAT? I just talked to Danielle yesterday."

"You won't be talking to her anymore." I started pacing the living room.

"Ain't no way someone went in the house and did that. Were my kids there? Are you sure she dead?"

"Positive. They had the nerve to show me a picture. Son, whoever you pissed off is coming back for you."

"I pissed off. You know Danielle had enemies." She smacked fire from my ass.

"I may not care for the bitch but she loved her kids. Do you really believe she'd jeopardize their well-being?"

"You're right." I let the palm of my hand run over my head.

"Rome, the person was like a thief in the night as the detective said. Its like the person was a ghost. No one saw anything." I stood there tryna wrap my mind around the story.

"I can't believe the nigga went back to finish the job." I said to myself but she heard me.

"What you talking about?" I blew my breath and got ready to tell the story and listen to her curse me out.

"Please tell me you're speaking of someone else named Kane, who had a daughter name Alexis." She said after hearing everything.

"Ma."

"OH MY GOD ROME!" Now she was pacing.

"I gotta get outta here."

"Ma, calm down."

"Calm down? Calm down?" She chuckled and not in a good way.

"Let me get this right. You pretended to love her just so you could get close to her father. Then, you shoot, kidnap and throw her outta a moving truck. Let's not forget the shot missed her father and impacted the mother."

"That's not her real mother." She stopped pacing and looked at me.

"A woman doesn't have to birth a child to be considered his or her mother. Let me tell you something. She got in my face.

"That woman raised Alexis since she was young and anyone who knew them, knew that. Don't ever downplay a woman's position as a mother just because she didn't come outta her pussy. What's wrong with you?" My mom was very sentimental about that because I had two foster sisters she loved dearly and considered them her own. She raised them since they were newborns and both of them are her kids.

"I don't know why you even thought to listen to that old woman and get yourself involved in this." She shook her head.

"Ma, he killed my father and..."

"SO WHAT? THE BASTARD DESERVED IT FOR MOLESTING THAT BABY."

"What?" She blew her breath.

"Rome, I never told you the exact reason he died, well got murdered but it's because he was sick."

"Don't say that ma."

"He was son. He met Erica, and somehow started touching her daughter."

"Why didn't her mom stop it?"

"She was on drugs real bad. When Kane found out, it took them a while to find him but when they did, I heard they tortured the fuck outta him and to be honest, it's exactly what he gets." I didn't say anything because Lexi said he did touch her at the hospital.

"And before you say it, they had all types of proof. Video footage of him tryna take her away and a bunch of other shit."

"Well they could've allowed him to live." I'm not sure why I said that because if anyone touched my kids, I'd probably do the same.

"I love you so much son but what you did is gonna get you killed. I'm surprised you're still alive." She went in my sisters' room and started packing bags for them while they were at school.

"What are you doing?"

"You may not have protected the kids mother but you won't leave me in the open to die. I'm taking my daughters and grandkids with me. If you wanna see them, call and I'll set up a spot."

"Ma."

"Get out Rome."

"Really?"

"Yes really. I can't believe you put us in a position to die. Just go." She was crying and pushing me out the door.

"I'm sorry ma. I'm gonna get them." She slammed the door in my face.

I didn't even attempt to go back. I went to my car and sped back to the hotel. I need to figure out a way to get that nigga. Whether my pops were wrong or not, he didn't have to kill him.

Crystal

After listening to Rome discuss this so called take down with Frankie and Lexi's father, I grabbed my things to go. See, everyone probably thinks I'm in love with Rome but it's far from the truth. Yes, he has a decent sex game but my eye has always been on Frankie and will stay that way.

The only problem is the Lexi bitch who just couldn't stay away. I mean if she had, I wouldn't be stalking my man the way I do. It's evident that he's only with her due to some promise they made as kids. If he really loved her he would've never slept with anyone else.

Then this Whitney bitch was talking like she tough as hell, knowing good and well SJ is gonna kill her the minute he gets his hands on her. I only know that because one of my associates works at the hospital and told me what went down.

She said Whitney came in there and tased SJ's new girlfriend. Now I'm not sure what went down prior to, but I do know everyone in the Anderson family crazy. Well not Lexi. She plays tough but she's really a punk. I know the reason she snuck me at the club is because her family were there and she knew they wouldn't let me hit her.

Anyway, my plan to kill Lexi hasn't changed, which is why I tried to run the bitch over. Imagine my surprise when her ass got outta the way in just enough time. That may not have hurt her but the facial expression after showing her the video, gave me enough satisfaction. If I stuck around longer, I may have saw the dumb bitch cry. Unfortunately, time wasn't on my side because I had more important things to do.

"Bitchhhhhhhhh. Where you been?" My hospital associate Wendy said. I never called anyone my friend because the truth is, no one in the world really had one. Bitches will say they your friend and stab you in the back. I'm good. I only came here because she asked me to meet her for drinks. Evidently, she had some gossip and hell yea I wanna know.

"Around. What's up?" I waved the bartender over and asked for a frozen Margarita.

"Bitch. How about the Anderson family lost their grandmother the other day?" I don't know why she was telling me but if she started with this family, the story must be good.

"Aww so sorry to hear that. NOT!" We started laughing. She knew about the nonsense with Lexi.

"Get this. Her two sons were arguing loud as hell and you'll never believe the shit I heard." The lady passed me my drink. I took a sip and handed her the money.

"What?"

"Ok, so evidently the Lexi bitch was sexually molested when she was young." I almost choked.

"Yes girl. And the guy who did it, is some guy who has a son named Rome.

"You lying." I said in disbelief. Now it was all making sense on why he wanted to get Lexi's father. He vaguely mentioned him doing something to kill her dad but never what his own father did that caused his death. I wouldn't tell anyone that shit either.

"If I'm lying, I'm dying." She took another sip of her drink and picked up a wing.

"But get this." I sat there anxiously waiting for more tea.

"Her grandmother set it up, for Rome to find Lexi and get close. Once he did, he was supposed kill her father's wife, who by the way took a bullet for the dad and almost died."

"Wait! I'm lost." There was so much shit going on in their family, I couldn't keep up with the story.

"Ok. From what I gathered, grandma hates the stepmother and she set it up to get her murdered. Lexi's father killed Rome's, years ago and he came back for revenge. He was Lexi's boyfriend and knew the entire time who she was. He aimed for the father, shot the stepmother and grandma set it all up."

"No fucking way." I sipped the rest of my drink and ordered another.

"So the bitch uses Frankie as her guardian angel. It explains why he feels the need to save her." She gave me a crazy look.

"What?"

"I don't think that's it at all."

"What you think it is then?"

"I've seen the way he is around her Crystal, and not only does he protect her but he's definitely in love."

"Psst." I waved my hand.

"I'm serious."

"Whatever."

"What you gonna do now? He's not going to leave her." She asked and offered me a wing.

"Yea Crystal. What you gonna do now?" I turned around and stared at Frankie and Kane Jr.

Frankie has always been sexy to me but for some reason, he looked extra scrumptious today. His denim jeans hung off his ass and the T-shirt was tucked a little in the front of his jeans. He had on a fresh pair of Jordan's and you could tell he just came from the barbershop. Kane Jr. was sexy as hell too but that nigga crazy. I didn't even wanna look at him. He might think I'm doing something wrong.

"Hey baby." I hopped off the seat and stood in front of him.

"Damn you fine." Wendy said.

"I know right?" Both of us sucked our teeth. Is he really conceited?

"Let me buy you a drink." Wendy was pressed for him but by the look on his face, you could tell he wasn't beat.

"Nah. My woman may not like it and beat yo ass."

"She ain't doing shit." He moved closer.

"You're right. I wouldn't even let her stoop to your level. I'll beat your ass though." He grabbed her by the hair and bent her neck back. Frankie was cracking up.

"All you had to do was say you're not interested." Wendy said with her face contorted due to how tight he had her hair in his hands.

"I could've but then this wouldn't be fun." He lifted her drink and poured it all over her. Wendy was mad as hell.

"Kane why would you do that?" I was curious as to why he did it too.

"You think I don't know you're the nurse bitch, my cousin knocked out in the hospital?" I had no idea what he was talking about.

"Don't ever disrespect his girl again or I'm not the one you'll have to worry about." He tossed her on the floor.

"You ready Frankie?" He asked and outta nowhere I felt hands on the back of my throat.

"Frankie what are you doing?" He leaned in to whisper in my ear.

"You're gonna explain why you led that nigga to my house, tried to run my fiancé over and showed her that fucking video." At that very moment, I knew he was about to kill me.

"Frankie, let's talk about this." His hand moved from my neck to my hair and he was basically dragging me out the place.

I used my hands to try and pry his off, scratched him and even tried to kick but nothing was working. Him and Kane were both staring at me because one of my shoes were off and my knee had blood dripping down. When I say he dragged me outta there, he really did. The crazy thing is, not one person intervened or even questioned him. What is this world coming to?

Frankie

"Get in." I pushed Crystals dumb ass in the truck I drove in.

"Frankie." She tried to speak and I used my hand to squeeze her cheeks. Her lips were poked out like a fish and the harder I did it, the more she cried. Ask me if I cared.

"Don't say my fucking name again." I pushed her back and listened to the back of her head hit the door. She should've gotten in when I told her to.

"I'll be behind you." Kane said and went over to his ride. The second, I received the call informing me where Crystal was, I sped over. She had been missing and I didn't wanna lose her.

The only reason Kane came is because he was with me at the dealership. Lexi's birthday is coming up and she wanted the brand-new BMW X3 i30 truck. I ordered it in jet black with chocolate interior. She was gonna be happy as hell since she's been eyeing it for a while now.

"Aight." I made sure the child lock was on the door and slammed it. I heard a scream and moved to the driver's side.

"Frankie where are you taking me?" Crystal whined, cried, begged and offered her pussy the entire ride to the warehouse. Oh yea, Ima take her life.

See, I was gonna let her live but when Lexi told me she was working with the Rome nigga, there was no other choice. Then to find out she tried to run her over and showed the video of her tryna fuck me outside the subway pissed me off even more. I knew then she'd cause more problems alive and knew she'd be better off dead. You can only give a person so many chances before their true colors come out.

It's not like I loved her, so me killing her isn't gone make me feel a certain way. In my eyes, she knew exactly what she was doing and should've expected this. The crazy part is we stood behind them as they spoke about whatever went down in the hospital room. I wasn't there but Lexi told me, and to hear the other bitch spreading the shit only pissed us off.

Yea, we knew who the Wendy bitch was because when Whitney tased Dree, she walked in the room popping shit. SJ knocked her out and paid one of the other nurses to get her information. We all sat outside her house a few times to find out who she lived with, if she had a man and any other thing we needed to know.

We all knew once Dree gave birth she was gonna return to the hospital and whoop her ass because that's just Dree. She's not one to let things slide. Anyway, SJ is holding on to the info for her. I'm sure the bitch thinks she's in the clear but it's far from the truth. Dree is gonna beat that ass when she delivers.

I parked my truck, snatched Crystal out, drug her inside and through the back door. There was a dirt road and a few cars.

"You ready?" I asked Eddie who had a grin on his face.

"Hell yea. I ain't never done no shit like this. I can't wait." You would think he won a million dollars from how excited he was.

"Ummmm, what's going on?" I sensed the nervousness and smiled.

"I'm gonna do to you, exactly what you tried to do to my girl." Her eyes grew big and she started shaking.

"Frankie please. I won't bother her anymore."

"Too late for regrets." I nodded and Todd gripped Crystal's arm. He took her for a walk down the dirt road.

"Yo, I'm about to tape this." Kane took his phone out.

"Make sure you go back and forth." I told Eddie and he told me not to worry, he had this. I backed up and so did everyone else.

"Frankie please." She started fighting with Todd. He literally held her by the throat in the air. Eddie revved the engine to the mustang up and smiled hard as hell.

"This nigga crazy." Kane said and got ready to record. I nodded and he sped off. Because Todd had her almost half a mile down, it took Eddie a good thirty seconds to reach her but just as he made it close, Todd dropped Crystal and moved out the way.

Once the car hit her, she flew in the air and landed on the ground. You heard the car go in reverse and we watched Eddie run her over. She looked like a crash test dummy as he did it over and over. Me and Todd had to yell at him to stop because one of her legs detached and her eyes were popping outta her head.

"Man, that shit is serious. Bring me someone else. I wanna do it again." This nigga had us cracking up.

"When we find Rome, you can do it." Him and Kane walked over to Crystal and surveyed the damage. It's sad I had to end her life but she's known for a while now never to fuck with my family and especially; not Lexi.

****

"What you doing sexy?" I wrapped my arm around Lexi as she stood in the bathroom mirror.

"Admiring my flat stomach because once the baby blows me up, that's it." I swung her around.

"You pregnant?"

"Not yet. I was just saying in general."

"Have you taken a test? I have been squirting all I had in you." She tossed her head back laughing.

"No. I have a gyn appointment in a week. I'll ask the doctor to take one then. And before you ask why, it's because the store tests aren't always accurate. I don't wanna get a false positive and get excited over nothing."

"I get it baby but, in my mind, you already are so make sure you eat for two and no stressing."

"Easy for you to say." I knew she was speaking about her family and this punk roaming free. Wherever he is, he's hiding well and I'd hate to be affiliated with him. Guilty or not, they all dying just like his baby mother did.

She thinks, I didn't recognize her at the hospital the night everything went down but I did. We were so caught up tryna find Lexi and figure out what went down with SJ and his dad, that I couldn't touch her the way I wanted.

Sadly, she met her demise as her kids slept in the other room. I slit her throat quickly along with the bitch next to her and disappeared in the night. One would think Rome would've hidden her or something but nope. She was in the very same house I shot her in.

I did call 911 and report a burglary. She had small kids and they wouldn't know what to do when they woke up. At least, the cops could take them to a relative. Hell, they need to get used to living without their parents anyway.

"I know you got a lot going on babe. Let me take care of you." I undid the belt to her robe and couldn't help but to lick my lips. My baby was bad in all areas. I'm mad as hell it took us so long to get it right but I do know we're gonna take forever making up. I lifted her on the sink and opened her legs.

"I love you so much Frankie." She moaned in my ear as I slid my index finger up and down her bottoms lips.

"I love you just as much babe." I kissed down her neck, caressed and sucked on her breasts but what I wanted was further below and she knew it. She lifted both knees to her chest, which gave me a much better view of what I wanted.

"Ssssss." My tongue took over for my fingers.

"You pretty as hell when you cum." I helped her off the sink after the third release and led her in the bedroom where we stayed all night.

****

"Who you think following my cousin?" I asked Kane Jr. when we pulled up to his house. Lexi was over her parents, so me and him went out to check on the spots and grab something to eat.

"I can't even tell you. I mean its one thing to get at her while she's far away from her parents but whoever it is, followed her back. If you ask me, its someone she knows. Did she have any boyfriends before me?" He opened the car door.

"Not anyone like you."

"Nigga, nobody will ever be like me." He cheesed hard as hell.

"Shut yo stuck up ass up."

"Whatever."

"But seriously, no. My uncle wasn't playing that shit. She went to school and came home. She did go to parties and stuff but there wasn't anyone specific in her life."

"Then, I can't think of who it could be."

"What happened with the license plates?"

"That shit went nowhere. Whoever drove the vehicle had it registered under a dead person."

"No shit." I was shocked.

"Yup, which also tells me this motherfucker smart as hell. He's definitely in the game or knows someone in it, to give him access to shit like that. Even the cameras were high tech. Shit, if he didn't fuck Raya's house up, we wouldn't have known they were there."

"You think he wanted y'all to know?" I asked because if he left them out in the open what other way is it to look at it?

"It's the way I'm looking at it. But why?" He opened the door and Raya was on the couch watching television.

"What yo sexy ass doing here?"

"Oh, I can't be here?" She questioned and folded her arms.

"You can be anywhere you want." He kissed her and before they started a R rated scene, I stopped them.

"I asked because you were supposed to be staying at your moms."

"Her and my dad wanted a date night, so I had him drop me off here. Oh, he said your house is nice and you have good taste."

"Tell him thanks, I guess."

"I told him, of course you had good taste because of me." She had the biggest smile on her face.

"You got damn right."

"I'm going in the basement to start the game." I left those two and went downstairs. Who the hell wants to see all that mushy shit? I guess, I see what he means when Lexi and I do it.

Lexi

I woke up this morning excited about attending the doctor's appointment. Ever since Frankie and I discussed it last week, we've both been extra happy. And let's not forget that even if I weren't last week, I most likely am this week.

The two of us been staying at the hotel so we could be alone. It's fun staying at my parents, his parents and my brothers place but we wanted alone time. Walking around naked and laying up the way we used to at home is all I want and if it has to be in this hotel, then so be it. The hotel is very nice and it's where SJ's been staying when he's not at my aunt's house so I see Dree and lil man here too sometimes.

I got out the shower and picked my phone up. It was my mom asking what time I'm coming to get her. She is as excited as we are and refuses to miss the first appointment. It's funny because I'm only going to my gynecologist. But like Frankie, she insists I'm pregnant and since this is gonna be the first grand baby, she wants to be there.

I sent her a text telling her I'll be there when I'm dressed. I put the phone on the nightstand, threw my clothes on and went down the small staircase. The smell of food invaded my nostrils. I followed it and saw Frankie sitting on the couch with my brother playing that stupid Fortnite game. I was so over it, that when the system went down to update for three hours I was in my glory. Him and a bunch of other people around the world seemed to be pissed but if you have anyone in your family who plays this game, anytime it shuts down, be happy.

"Which one is mine?" I asked and got no answer. I walked over and stood in front of the television.

"Which food container is mine?" Frankie licked his lips while my brother sucked his teeth.

"You can have whatever you want. Damn, you sexy. Come here." I moved closer and he stood.

"I want you." He dropped the remote on the seat and had my hand in his.

"After the doctors Frankie." He stopped and looked at me.

"I promise to suck that dick so good, you'll be ready for a nap."

"Now how am I supposed to go on with the rest of my day after hearing that?"

"Because you know your fiancé is the shit and if I say something, I'm gonna do it." I lifted the lid on one of the containers and placed a piece of bacon in my mouth.

"You coming to the doctors, right?" He leaned in to kiss me.

"Yea. I'll be there." We were gonna drive together but as you can see, he's stuck on the damn game.

"Let me go get my mom and I'll see you soon. Oh and Frankie." He was on his way back to play the game.

"Make sure you drop him off. He doesn't like to hear us moaning." We both busted out laughing.

"I swear to God Lexi, you better go head." Kane, like any sibling hated to hear anything about sex regarding me. I get a kick outta bothering him though.

"Love you brother." I blew him a kiss.

"LEXI!" Frankie shouted when I opened the door.

"Yes baby."

"Stop tryna outrun the security." I busted out laughing. Him and my family were so worried about Rome finding me, they hired security to watch me. A few times I tried to shake him but it was no use because he was on it. When he told them, they were all mad at me.

"Alright."

"Lexi."

"I heard you Frankie." I closed the door and left. I'm not gonna try and lose them today anyway. My mom is still moving slow and my father and brother would kill me if I did.

****

"Well Ms. Anderson. You are indeed pregnant." The doctor said after they tested my urine

"YES!" Frankie shouted and my mom smiled.

"Would you like to see how far along you are?"

"Yup." I didn't have to open my mouth because him and my mom answered every question. The nurse brought in the machine and come to find out, I'm going on two weeks.

"Damn, I got you pregnant the same day your cast came off." My mom sucked her teeth.

"My bad, Mrs. April." He started laughing. The doctor showed our baby on the machine and allowed us to hear the heartbeat. Frankie's crazy ass had the nerve to ask if he could tell what we were having.

"Sorry, we won't know that until she's at least four or five months." He was disappointed but told him he'd pay extra to check every month.

"I'm so fucking happy Lexi." He hugged me tight. My mom was in the hallway on the phone telling my dad. She was already trying to baby shop.

"I am too. I love you." We started kissing.

"Alright you two. I'm hungry." My mom said.

"You coming?"

"Nah, I got some things to handle. I'll see you at home." He kissed my cheek and walked us outside.

"Where you wanna eat?"

"Anywhere honey." My dad called again to say congratulations and check on us. They were so overprotective and I thought it would bother me but it doesn't.

I pulled up at TGIF Friday's and helped my mom get out. She walked slow but I have no problem helping her. I opened the door and waited for the lady to seat us.

"I'm happy you and Frankie got it together." My mom smiled looking over the menu. Everyone wanted us married with kids already.

When I showed her my ring, she cried. My father said it was about time and I never should've wasted my energy on anyone else knowing Frankie is the man I wanted. I tried to explain he had someone else too but like he said, he was buying time with the ho. My mom told him to stop saying that and he'd just wave her off.

"Me too ma. I'm not sure if I wanna wait until after the baby or hurry up and get it over with since we've waited so long."

"It's whatever you want Lexi. We all know that man will walk down the aisle with you tomorrow if you want." I put my head down grinning. Frankie would drop everything to do just that.

"Are you ladies ready to order?" The waitress asked and disappeared to put it in.

My mom and I stayed in the restaurant for almost two hours eating and talking. Frankie and my dad were having a fit because they had no idea why it took us so long. They said if we weren't home soon, one of them was coming to get us.

"I'll be right back Lexi." My mom stood.

"Where you going?"

"The bathroom."

"You want me to come with you?"

"No, it's ok. Here's the money for the food and make sure your dads food is right. I don't wanna hear his mouth." We ordered for him and my siblings. Frankie ate already but I still brought food home in case. I walked up to the register, grabbed the bags and waited for my receipt. I had my head down and looked up to see my mom returning from the bathroom. The look on her face told me something wasn't right and when the person popped up behind her, I knew then shit was about go left.

The lady handed me the receipt and stepped away from the register. I left everything on the counter and went to my mother. I'm pregnant and definitely shouldn't be fighting but this motherfucker is about to make me show how my hands work.

"I don't care which one of you do it, or how you get it. But what I do know is, you got twenty minutes to call your father and tell him to bring me ten million dollars or not only is this bitch dead, but the cops will find out what happened in that hospital room." My mouth hung open. How the fuck did anyone know about my grandmother? No one was in the room with us.

"Nineteen minutes and counting." It wasn't until we stepped out the door that I noticed the gun behind my mother's back. Outta nowhere a car sped in the parking lot and stopped directly in front of us. The windows were tinted so we couldn't see inside. But when the doors opened my heart stopped and my mom reached for me. How did he find me?

SJ

"I'll be back in a few Dree and lil man, make sure you ready for me on the game." He balled his fist up and pushed it against mine.

They been staying with me off and on until I get a new place. It's fun and I couldn't for the life of me understand how a man didn't make time to spend with their seed. Not only is he smart for a kid who just turned five but he was well mannered. He also knew his limit when it came to his mom and you could tell how much he loved her.

"Got it. Bye SJ." He hopped out and ran in the house.

"SJ, please be careful." Dree stared at me with those big brown eyes. She knew Whitney contacted me about an hour ago asking if we could meet up. Dree didn't want me to go because she felt it was another set up but I had something for her ass if it was.

"I'm not leaving you baby." I pulled her closer and gently kissed her.

"Call someone else to go with you."

"Dree, I love how concerned you are but I got this."

"Fuck that. I'm coming." She pouted and folded her arms across her chest. I stepped out, went to her side and carried her in the house. She ain't about to punk me the way she did Herb. And I would never allow her in harm's way.

"What happened to her?" I heard her mom shout and come running over. By the looks of it, you would think the same way. Dree was holding my neck extra tight and telling me no, she wasn't letting go. Her pops came in the room and nodded.

"She good."

"Then what's all this for?"

"J, you know your daughter extra when he leaves." She sucked her teeth as I laid Dree on the couch.

"SJ."

"I'll be fine Dree." She kept shaking her head no. I loved this woman with all my heart but I'll never go if I stayed here.

"I'm out." Her brother Dreek said coming outta the back. We spoke and he disappeared.

"Am I missing something?" Her mom asked.

"Not that I know of." I said and backed away from my girl before she wrapped her arms around me again. I understood her concern and it was killing me to see her so upset but I had to get this bitch and she knew it.

"I'll be back Dree."

"SJ!" She shouted.

"Make sure you feed my baby." Her father locked eyes with me and closed the door.

I ran to my truck, typed in the destination Whitney gave me that was an hour away and sparked a blunt. I needed to be calm. I wasn't gonna smoke the whole thing because I had to be alert too in case shit goes left. There's no telling what Whitney has up her sleeve and if I know her, she'll definitely wanna fuck too.

I never told Dree about the messages she sent me. Even after the fiasco at the hospital when she tased my girl, she was still trying. I mean she sent explicit text messages along with video ones. Then, she had a few of her crying and telling me how much she loved me and if I didn't play with her heart, she would've never tried to kill me. I also got some threatening ones, which I kept so when I do take her life, shit is justified. Say what you want, but I like to keep my track record clean.

I pulled up at the house and her car was the only one there. It didn't mean shit but I'll give her the benefit of the doubt. I cut the truck off, sent her a message saying I was outside and grabbed the small carry bag I had. It had the items in it I needed and I'm sure it won't be enough time to run back and get it out. I glanced around the spot and it appeared to be a quiet area but I'm not from this spot so I had no idea if it were or not. There were no houses around and it made my reason for coming here even better.

"Hey baby." She had on one of those negligee things. This time my dick didn't get hard.

"What up?" I stepped in the door and she had some romantic shit going on. Candles, music and all that. I stood at the kitchen staring at the food she cooked. This bitch reminded me of Lynn Whitfield in, A Thin Line Between Love and Hate. It's like no matter what I said about us being over, she wasn't getting.

"SJ, let me start off by saying I apologize for everything. I just wanted us to be together." She wrapped her arms around my neck.

"It's all good. What you cook?" I moved her arms and checked the pots. I looked on the side of the sugar jar and noticed a small vial. She has to be the stupidest bitch I know. Who tries to drug someone and leaves the evidence out in the open?

"I made you some steak, potatoes and green beans." I admit it smelled good and whether I saw the vial or not, I wouldn't eat it.

"Where's the bathroom?" She pointed upstairs. I still had my bag on my side and took it up with me.

Instead of going in the bathroom, I went in the bedroom and this bitch had handcuffs and toys in here. I guess she had big plans for us. Too bad, Dree and I do way more shit to each other and it's much better.

I dumped the stuff out and prepared it all to make sure everything was perfect. It's not going to look like an accident but it will when I place this suicide note here. I typed it up and forged her signature. I saw her sign shit a million times and even though it ain't perfect, what I did was close enough.

"YO, WHITNEY. COME HERE." I shouted at the top of the steps. She sashayed her ass up and made sure to switch the entire way. I smiled and escorted her in.

"I see you has shit set up for us." I pointed to the handcuffs in my hand.

"I did." She ran her hands up my chest.

"How about we skip dinner and start now?" She removed the thin robe and I pushed her on the bed.

"Let's start with these cuffs." She smiled and allowed me to put them on her with no questions asked. It was now clear as day, that she was in love with me. I mean who would let a man do this knowing he said he was gonna kill you?

"I missed you so much baby." She opened her legs and stared at me. I pretended to unbuckled my jeans.

"Give it to me baby."

"Close your eyes while I pour this massage oil on you." She did like I asked.

I placed the gloves on my hand and grabbed the small can of gasoline. It was in one of those small paint cans you get from Home Depot. I had it in a freezer bag zipped up to keep the smell down.

I poured it on her legs slowly to give it the feeling of being lotion. It didn't take long for her to notice the difference.

"Why does it smell like gasoline?"

"Because I'm about to set yo ass on fire." Her eyes popped open. I only planned on giving her a bullet to her head but once Frankie told me what he did to Crystal. I felt it was only fair to make her feel what would've happened to me if she succeeded with the cocktail and if I got caught in the house when she tried it burn it down.

"SJ, please take these handcuffs off me." She was squirming, wiggling and doing any and everything tryna get out.

"Nah. You said, you missed me and wanted to fuck."

"SJ, stop playing." I took my gun out and shot her in the leg. Her scream only intensified the pleasure I received seeing her in pain. Tears were flooding her face and blood began to pour out.

"I'm gonna let you feel what I would've felt when you tried to burn me alive. The shot is for whoever helped you that night but trust, I'm gonna get that motherfucker too." I flipped the lighter.

"SJ, please." She cried out.

"Remember you set my house on fire while I slept?" She didn't say anything.

"Have fun with Crystal and save room for everyone who helped you." I let the flame touch the comforter and watched as the fire overtook her body. Watching her flesh burn is pretty nasty and I didn't feel bad. I couldn't because had I not shot through the windshield, it would've been me.

Once the room engulfed in flames, I let the rest of the gasoline fall on the rug until it ran out. It's just a matter of time before the entire house burned. And because this house is in a secluded area, it would take a while for someone to report it.

I made sure I had everything and placed the suicide letter under a rock close to the house. It was in a red envelope so it won't be missed when the cops came on the property. I walked to my truck and had this aching feeling that something was wrong with Lexi. I pulled my phone out to call her but something or should I say someone, stopped me.

"What's up now nigga?" I felt the steel on the back of my head.

"Herb?" I questioned.

"Damn right it's me. How's it feel to know I'm about to take your life, for ruining mine?" I heard the gun cock.

Did I really let this cornball catch me slipping?

Raya

"You ready ma?" Kane asked and carried me to the car. I had a doctor's appointment to see if my arm and leg healed. I prayed they did because this carrying me shit was getting on my nerves. I wanted to walk and have sex with my man, who refused until I had at least one cast off. I can't even lie; I've tried many times and he will not budge. Talking about he likes to do a lot and he ain't got time to hear me complaining.

"Yea. I can't wait to get these casts off."

"Me too. I love the way you give me head but I need to feel inside."

"And I can't wait for you to do it." He bit down on his lip and I all I wanted was for him to lay me down and make love to me.

"Let's get you to the doctor." He lifted and carried me to the truck. After he placed the seatbelt on, he locked his house up and jumped in the driver's side.

"Ima need you to ride the fuck outta me when you get this leg cast off." He squeezed my upper thigh and drove off. I couldn't help but laugh. He was definitely a piece of work, said whatever is on his mind and yet; I was deeply and irrevocably in love with him.

It could be his bluntness or sexiness. Whatever the case, he's all mine and now that my parents know about him, I'm showing him off any chance I get.

"Yea, I'll be there when I finish at the doctors with Raya." I heard Kane say on the phone. He hung up and pulled in the parking lot at the office.

He went inside, retrieved a wheelchair and returned with a smile on his face. I opened the door with my good hand and for some reason felt as if someone were watching me. The feeling was so strong, it made me scared about getting out.

"What's wrong?" I surveyed the parking lot and no one was there.

"Nothing. I'm ok." I gave him a smile and waited for him to place me in the chair. The closer we got to the door, the feeling went away.

"You sure?"

"Yea. Oh and if you need to leave, it's ok."

"Nah, it was my mother. She wants to see me."

"Go head baby. My mom is meeting me here so I won't be alone."

"It's fine Raya." His phone started ringing again.

"Kane, no one knows I'm here. I'll be fine baby."

"You tryna get rid of me?" I laughed and told him no. I know his mom is still recovering and he was a mama's boy. I didn't wanna be the girlfriend who kept him away from his family.

"You sure?" He asked when I told him again to go check on her.

"Yea. My mom just sent a text saying she's on her way." I showed her message to him and he seemed to be ok.

"Aight. Call me when you're finished." He kissed my lips and walked out. The minute he did, the eerie feeling of someone watching me returned. No one came in after us so I wasn't sure as to why.

I waited for the nurse to call my name. Once she did, she came out and pushed me to the back. There were others in the rooms and I couldn't help but wonder where my mom was.

Knowing her, she stopped to grab a coffee or something. I sent her a text when the nurse left the room. She said she wasn't coming because she figured Kane was there.

"Ma, I told Kane it was ok to leave because you were coming." I said to my mom on the phone when I called her.

"I'm sorry honey. Your dad wanted to go out for lunch. Do you want us to come?"

"No. I'll send Kane a message to come back." We conversed for a few more minutes and hung up. I hurried to call Kane because something was off. He didn't answer and it made me worry. I called back three more times.

"Hey, Ms. Hollis." The doctor said and started his exam.

By the time he finished, an hour had passed and the cast on my leg was removed and he placed a smaller one on my arm. I was so excited because I could walk and do things on my own. He said one of the nurses would return with all my paperwork and new appointment date. I started to text Kane to see if he was in the waiting room when the door opened. I looked up expecting to see the doctor but this man was far from that.

"What are you doing here?" I looked back down at my phone to send the message but he snatched the phone out my hand. I hadn't seen him in a while and he shows up here taking my shit. Who the hell did he think he was?

"What you mean why am I here? I'm always around." He locked the door and moved closer. I didn't even know these offices had locks.

"Excuse me!"

"Raya, don't act like we don't have history." He had his hand on my face.

"MOVE!" His hands were now on the side of the chair with his face about to touch mine.

"How could you sleep with that nigga? I was supposed to be your first. Then you dressed sexy and performed for him." My entire body froze when he said that.

"Have you... Have you been watching me?" I was scared for the answer but needed to hear it.

"I've been watching you for a very long time Raya."

To Be

Continued...

A Note to My Readers

I want to say THANK YOU a million times to each and every one of you. A lot of you have been rocking with me from the very beginning.

I love y'all and I am more than grateful.

For all the new readers, I love y'all too for taking a chance on a different author. I know it's hard to read and even like new authors when you're stuck on specific ones. My writing may not be the same as your favorite author but I put my all into my work just the same and it's greatly appreciated to know you took a chance.

Again, this is Urban Fiction and as an author, we have the freedom to write the way we want and shouldn't be ridiculed because the book

isn't written the way you think it should be,

ended the way you wanted, or whatever reason

you can think of. However, I'm going to

continue writing and entertaining everyone to

the best of my ability.

Sending all of you a million hugs, kisses and

thanks. I hope you enjoy this series.

CPSIA information can be obtained
at www.ICGtesting.com
Printed in the USA
LVHW02s2146010818
585625LV00023B/368/P